MW01135102

THE CHIMERA

BLACK FORCE SHORTS BOOK TWO

MATT ROGERS

Join the Reader's Group and get a free 200-page book by Matt Rogers!

Sign up for a free copy of '**HARD IMPACT**'.
Meet Jason King — another member of Black Force.

Experience King's most dangerous mission — action-packed insanity in the heart of the Amazon Rainforest.

No spam guaranteed.

Just click here.

BOOKS BY MATT ROGERS

THE JASON KING SERIES

Isolated (Book 1)

Imprisoned (Book 2)

Reloaded (Book 3)

Betrayed (Book 4)

Corrupted (Book 5)

Hunted (Book 6)

THE JASON KING FILES

Cartel (Book 1)

Warrior (Book 2)

Savages (Book 3)

THE WILL SLATER SERIES

Wolf (Book 1)

Lion (Book 2)

BLACK FORCE SHORTS

The Victor (Book 1)

The Chimera (Book 2)

Washington D.C.

L ars Crawford had come to learn many things over the three years he'd spent as a black operations handler.

The opportunity, at the time, had been impossible to resist. His work for the Department of Defence had grown stale — most of his focus, involving research into human reaction speed in combat, had settled into a monotonous process of repetition. You could only do so much investigation before your subconscious gnawed at you, pleading for your life's work to be put into practice. Lars had spent many, many years arguing for a division of solo operators, demonstrating through endless presentations to his superiors that sometimes a gifted soldier came along who needed to work alone.

Three years ago, his requests had finally been granted.

Ever since then, his life had been a whirlwind.

Sometimes he found himself grateful for the opportunity. Sometimes he could savour the thrill of sending his operators into some of the most dangerous situations on the planet, because he had full faith in their abilities to succeed.

And other times — like right now — he found himself so overwhelmed by events that were unfolding, so horrified and hopeless and unsettled, that he felt as if the world was set to come crashing down all around him.

This time, it just might be...

He sat in the windowless room with his head in his hands, taking a vital moment to compose himself before the upper echelon of military commanders entered and he was forced to put his game face on. Stress leeched from his bones, leaking into the atmosphere. It was palpable. He could taste it. He wasn't sure how — when the party of officials stormed in minutes from now — he would manage to act like there was nothing out of the ordinary.

Ridiculous.

He didn't need to pretend all was well, because everyone in the room would understand that shit had truly hit the fan.

By this point he associated visits to the White House with mind-boggling stress. Black Force — the division he'd run for nigh on a thousand consecutive days — had its own headquarters several miles out of the city centre. He was only ever summoned into the bowels of this enormous building when situations transpired that were unimaginably sensitive.

Like his current predicament.

The door opened and three men entered wordlessly — there was no need for flippant greetings or unnecessary conversation starters. All of the group operated in a world with zero margin for error. There was no point exchanging pleasantries. The trio sat facing Lars across the undecorated room and they got straight down to business.

'The informant wasn't bullshitting?' Lars said. 'That's what I'm getting from all this.'

One of the men — a balding man in his early fifties — piped up. 'It appears to be heading that way.'

'How quickly is it heading that way? Because if any of this is in any way plausible, then we needed to act yesterday.'

'If it's really happening in Bhutan, then there's not much we can do about it in a hurry.'

'You think that was deliberate?' Lars said. 'Setting up their camp in one of the least accessible places on earth?'

'Probably. I'd say that's what they were going for. They need that window to pack up their stuff and flee if they notice suspicious activity.'

'So we can't do anything,' Lars said, a lump forming in his throat.

Bhutan, with a population just edging over seven hundred thousand, had little going for it in terms of international terrorism hotspots. That had all changed when the informant had arrived in the United States weeks earlier. At first they'd labelled his ramblings as the spouting of a deranged lunatic, but even the most preliminary of investigations had revealed that he might be telling the truth. The days had unfolded, and piece by piece the evidence had been uncovered — most of it coming in the way of discrepancies in the flight logs.

Lars had been over everything what felt like a thousand times by this point.

He didn't need reminding.

He needed an action plan.

He dissipated some of the tension in his body by slapping an open palm against the wood surface of the table in front of him. One of the military officials jolted — Lars looked across and recognised the familiar face of the National Security Advisor. His life had become so fast-paced that he barely stopped to register who he was talking to anymore.

'Okay,' Lars said, taking a deep breath. 'So this threat could be very real. So far, the flight logs don't add up. That could mean anything...'

'Well, the monastery is exactly where he said it was. We tapped into a couple of satellites over the region.'

Lars went pale. 'You sure?'

'Positive.'

'Jesus Christ, this is bad. And it's a logistical nightmare.'

The man in the middle — who Lars couldn't remember if he'd met before — piped up. 'We might have a solution.'

'Who are you?'

'That doesn't matter,' the guy said, and he flashed Lars a dark look that could only mean he was someone unimaginably important. 'What matters is that I have contact with Delta. Does the name Colt Griffin ring a bell?'

Lars looked toward the first man he'd been speaking to — the only one who held a position within Black Force's ranks. 'Is that the guy we were looking at?'

'Yes,' the mysterious second man said, even though the question hadn't been directed at him. Lars sensed irritation in his tone. 'You're the reason he's in Bhutan, as a matter of fact.'

'Why the hell is he in Bhutan?' Lars said.

'Because, apparently, you and your group of lone wolves were interested in him, which meant we couldn't send him into the field ... even though he held some of the best results we've ever seen in our Operator Training Course.'

'That's what we do,' Lars said, equally irritated. 'We

recruit the best of the best. That doesn't explain why he's in South Asia.'

'Soul searching. Finding himself. Who the hell knows.'

'Why isn't he with you?'

'Because transitioning from the Delta Force to the shadows of your organisation puts my men in a state of limbo. Right now he's not officially employed by anyone. So I don't know why you're asking me the questions. You're the one who ordered it.'

'So he's on vacation?'

'Not really. We told him to go home to his family and friends and let them know he might be taking an extended trip. Yes, I know I wasn't supposed to do that. But I've handed two of my men over to you before and I never heard from them again.'

Lars paused. 'You think they're dead?'

'I don't know what to think.'

'They're still alive. But I don't think you understand the sensitivity of what we do. And none of this adds up. Why did Griffin decide to go to Bhutan of all places? And isn't it awfully convenient that it lines up with the intel we just got? How do we know he's not involved?'

The mysterious guy simply shrugged. 'All good questions. None of which I can answer. You'll have to ask him yourself. He's in your hands.'

'He's our only option?'

The first man said, 'He's the only link we have in-country. He's the only one who could pull anything off within a twenty-four hour window.'

'He's one guy,' Lars said.

'I thought that was your specialty,' the second man sneered.

Lars sighed. 'I'll make the call.'

2

C olt Griffin didn't quite know what he was doing in Bhutan.

In fact, he hadn't been aware of the country's existence a couple of weeks earlier.

The last portion of his life had been filled with uncertainty, and all the secrets and withheld information had reached a fever pitch when his superiors had called him into a room and told him he was being released from the Delta Force, effective immediately. Flabbergasted and hurt, he'd predictably made a fuss. Eventually, his commanding officer had felt enough pity to quietly inform Griffin that the results of his Operator Training Course were being closely looked at by a secret division of the United States military. He'd been told to make peace with his past life and prepare for an extended detour through the world of black operations — that is, if he was up for the challenge.

He couldn't think of anything else he'd rather do.

For the past couple of weeks he'd been mulling over what his superiors had said. He'd been told to report to Washington D.C. on March 15th for an official offer, and everything other than that had been shrouded in secrecy. He knew almost nothing about what was going to take place, but he took solace in the fact that he should know *literally* nothing.

Command had been generous in hinting at his future.

There was the potential that he was heading for great things.

And that was all he needed.

Family was a moot point, but his superiors didn't know that. So when they'd told him to go make peace with his past — effectively hinting that whatever lay in his future was akin to a death sentence — he hadn't felt the need to go back to the hellhole town he'd grown up in. They were the reason he'd fled to the military. He'd do great things without them ever knowing, and that would prove himself more of a man than his father ever could have been.

Which was how he'd ended up with a two week window to go and do whatever the hell he wanted, granted that he wound up in Washington at the end of his travels. He'd thrown a dart across his tiny studio apartment at a world map poster and it had landed in Bhutan, a portion of South Asia he couldn't say he was familiar with.

But Griffin never half-assed anything, or went back on a promise.

He'd packed a bag with the bare essentials, bought a one-way ticket, and now he found himself here.

He sat at the edge of a sweeping field of grass, his back to a waist-high wooden fence running the entire perimeter of the property. He didn't know whose farm it was, or whether he was welcome loitering around its outskirts. He simply needed a place to sit and eat and think. He chewed on a mouthful of *jasha maru,* savouring the warm chicken stew. He'd bought it from a food cart a mile down the road and carried the wooden bowl to a quieter section of the Paro Valley.

Granted, everything was quiet out here.

But that was what he needed.

He didn't know much about his future, but he assumed that soon his life would be hell.

A voluntary hell, of course, considering the fact that he would lay down his life for his country.

But hell all the same.

If someone asked him what he was doing here, Griffin would struggle to come up with a cohesive answer. His brain had said *go,* and he had obliged. A week ago he'd been in Texas, and now he was in one of the more alien, beautiful regions on the planet.

He'd always been spontaneous.

He finished the meal and spent a moment soaking in the scenery. There'd been plenty of time for that in the Paro Valley, but he hadn't yet become accustomed to it.

The rural trail he'd been strolling down for the past hour was situated at the very bottom of the valley, a flat expanse of farmland dotted with clusters of civilisation. Towns materialised every few miles. Picturesque mountain ranges ran into the distance, most of them draped in low clouds and shrouded in mist. Lush sloping walls of green boxed him in on all sides, leading to destinations unknown. Griffin hadn't even bothered to consider venturing into the mountains. As far as he could tell, it was a death wish. They were inhospitable and sparsely populated and dangerous to the uninitiated.

Although the temperature was relatively cool, sweat

leeched from Griffin's pores, largely due to the intense humidity. It certainly had nothing to do with his physical fitness. The six-month Operator Training Course he'd gone through in the Delta Force had put him in the best shape of his life. He was fresh out of the program, which had thrust him into a state of limbo as he wondered what the offer would consist of.

He hadn't found out a thing about the nature of his results. Those had been kept resolutely hidden. But they were no doubt being scrutinised, because every other participant in the training course had continued down the usual route to becoming a Delta Force operative. Griffin had seen nothing of them since he'd been carted into that tiny office and told what was happening.

He got to his feet and slung his hiking backpack over his shoulders, clipping the chest strap across his pectorals. It was roughly a five-mile trek back to the small room he was renting in a budget hotel near the Paro Airport. He'd been strolling aimlessly around the Paro Valley for the better part of a week now, and in the back of his mind the knowledge that he would need to return stateside hovered ominously. Part of him wanted to disappear into South Asia and never return.

But he had potential, and that carried with it a burden.

He had a responsibility to fight.

Especially if the results of his Operator Training Course were as special as they'd been hinted.

He set off at a leisurely pace, with no pressing need to be anywhere. After a half hour of trudging along the gravel he passed back through the same tiny village he'd visited some time earlier, returning the now-empty wooden bowl to the food vendor along the way. The Bhutanese man with deep wrinkles etched into his forehead nodded, offering a warm smile.

Griffin returned the smile.

He had no reason not to.

He was young. He had his entire career in front of him. His ascent through the ranks of the United States military had been faster than anticipated, and it seemed after this brief detour in Bhutan he would be accepting even more responsibility.

His life, relatively speaking, was good.

Then he reached the opposite end of the village, passing huts and a handful of stone-walled retail stores selling fresh produce and other goods, and passed by an archaic wired payphone coated in rust. The entire thing had seemingly fallen into disrepair years ago. Griffin took one glance at it and determined that it no longer worked. Not that he had anyone to contact in the first place. He certainly didn't want to speak to his family.

He continued along the trail, passing the payphone.

It rang.

3

Something about the harsh shrilling pouring out of the rusting speaker set Griffin on edge.

On top of that, the timing unnerved him.

He didn't believe in coincidences.

He took a long look in either direction, as if hoping a stranger would materialise out of nowhere and answer the call. But there was no-one in sight. Griffin was as alone as it was possible to be. He didn't move, listening to the discordant *ring-ring, ring-ring* cutting through the peaceful silence of the valley. He wasn't sure what the hell would happen next, but he figured he might as well pick up the phone.

The alternative was wondering what it could be for the rest of his life.

So he trudged the few steps across the gravel and lifted the rusting receiver off its cradle. He pressed it to his ear.

Silence.

'Hello?' he said.

More silence.

'Hello?'

'I take it I'm speaking to Colt Griffin.'

Griffin hoped no-one had eyes on him at that exact moment, for the blood drained from his face in an instant. Even though a faint voice had told him the call was for him, he hadn't truly believed it. He'd been expecting either the static associated with a malfunctioning payphone, or a quick burst of unintelligible Dzongkha — the native language of Bhutan — followed by the person at the other end of the line hanging up.

He certainly hadn't been expecting an American voice.

'You are,' Griffin said, hesitant to divulge anything.

'I apologise for the nature of this call,' the voice at the other end of the line said. 'But I don't believe you took your phone to Bhutan, did you?'

'No, I didn't.'

'Was that deliberate?'

'Sure was.'

'You haven't asked who you're speaking to.'

'I imagine you'll tell me,' Griffin said. 'In due time. No point trying to force it out of you.'

'My name's Lars Crawford.'

'I'm going to need a bit more information than that.'

'I know. In due time.'

'You want something from me?'

'Yes, actually,' Lars said. 'I want to recruit you.'

Griffin paused. *Was this what his superiors had been referring to?*

A job offer from a division of the military that officially did not exist.

Why the hell was it coming in the form of an anonymous call to a Paro Valley payphone?

'This is a strange way of going about it,' Griffin said.

'I know. Trust me, I'd rather do it some other way. I get the sense you know something about me?'

'A little.'

'Well, that's good. Even though you're not supposed to know a thing. This might come as less of a shock if you have a rough idea of where you're headed.'

'I'm supposed to be in Washington soon,' Griffin said. 'Can't this wait?'

'I wish it could.'

'You need me now?'

'Pretty much.'

'I can be on the first flight out.'

'No. I need you in Bhutan.'

'You might want to start explaining what you're on about, or I'll hang up this phone and carry on my way. I have no way of knowing if you are who you say you are.'

'You hang up this phone and you'll be directly responsible for ignoring a bioterrorism threat. Right now you're the only chance we have of preventing it.'

Griffin paused. 'Go on.'

'I'm the chief handler for the division known as Black Force. I feel like we should start there.'

'Never heard of it.'

'That's kind of the point.'

'You're interested in me?'

'Yes.'

'Why?'

'The results of your Operator Training Course in the Delta Force.'

'Thought as much. What was so special about them?'

'Your reflexes and reaction speed, mostly. You're an all-around excellent soldier, but your ability to react quickly and intuitively is off the charts. Your brain processes events in a live combat situation at an astronomical rate.'

It sounded like Lars was reading directly off a fact sheet. Griffin grew restless. 'That's it? You're going to bring me into this black operations unit because of my reaction speed? I guess I always thought there was more to it than that.'

'That's the foundation of an indestructible soldier,' Lars said, and Griffin sensed intense passion in the man's voice. He wondered if Lars had specific expertise in this field. It certainly sounded as much. 'Everything you do is based off how fast you can react to situations on the fly. And I don't run a unit. I run a batch of independent, solo operatives. Those who can react at the speed of light stay alive. It's as simple as that. And it's better if they're alone in the field, so they don't have to be responsible for anyone else. If you can retaliate in the blink of an eye but your fellow soldiers can't, it'll only hold you back. That's the basis of what we do here. And, on March 15th, I was prepared to offer you a position in our ranks.'

'It's not March 15th,' Griffin noted.

'It certainly isn't.'

'And you're calling me on a payphone.'

'Desperate times. Desperate measures.'

'What do you need?'

'That can't be summed up in a few sentences. I need to break this down to you, and you need to listen to every word I say.'

'I can do that.'

'Right now, there's some serious shit going on in the mountains around the Paro Valley.'

'Look,' Griffin said, interrupting. 'I get it. You need to test me or something. Just come out and say it — I'd rather you be honest with me. You really expect me to believe there's some terrorist threat unfolding in South Asia, and I just happen to conveniently be here?'

'No, I don't expect you to believe it,' Lars said. 'Cause I hardly fucking believe it myself. And, trust me, I'd rather we had anyone else. You're untested in the field, if we're being honest. But you need to understand this isn't a drill. This is life or death. And you can turn me down, but you'll never hear from me or my organisation again.'

'Okay. Go on.'

'What are you doing in Bhutan?'

'Soul searching.'

'Cut the shit.'

'Okay. I threw a dart at a map.'

'I said—'

'I know what you said. You're just going to have to believe me, because it's the truth.'

'You don't know anything about what's going on?'

'No.'

'You haven't received any illicit job offers in that part of the world?'

'No.'

'You're not currently working for a paramilitary force, off the books?'

'No. And I suggest you get explaining if this is as serious as you say it is.'

Griffin sensed Lars hesitating on the other end of the line, and he wondered how ridiculous the following sentences would sound. He was expecting madness, but nothing could have prepared him for what followed.

'Okay,' Lars said, taking a deep breath to compose himself. 'Right now, the U.S. government is under the impression that a rogue paramilitary organisation has been holed up in an abandoned monastery for the better part of six months, paying a group of scientists obscene quantities of money to smash a few pathogens together into a chimera virus more deadly than anything ever manufactured.'

Griffin said nothing.

Suddenly, the air got a whole lot colder.

4

'I, uh...' Griffin said, staring into the distance at the nearest mountain range, draped in cloud and hovering ominously in the Bhutanese sky. 'I don't know what to say.'

'If I were you I'd be calling bullshit.'

'You sound like you're about to have a heart attack,' Griffin said. 'So I assume it's not bullshit.'

'It's not.'

'A paramilitary force?'

'We have to go off what our informant is telling us.'

'Who's the informant?'

'Ex-U.S. military. He was taking any job he could get after he got dishonourably discharged — morals be damned. Ended up roped into this scheme with a party of fourteen other mercenaries and spent a couple of months as a low-level grunt patrolling the monastery's perimeter before he finally discovered what was going on and fled back to America.'

'You going to go easy on him?'

'Probably not. He confessed to a lot of shit before he even stepped foot in Bhutan. He's an unsavoury character... to put it mildly.'

'So what makes you think he's telling the truth?'

'We didn't. For weeks. All of it sounded like a bunch of made up horse shit, but then we started taking a closer look at the Paro Airport, and none of it looks good.'

'What do you mean?'

'The flight logs, for starters. They don't add up. There's a different number of planes coming in every day based on which report you read, and there's a different quantity of cargo being offloaded from each incoming delivery. All of it points toward a cover-up. And the monastery the guy was rambling about exists. We scoured the satellites and found the fortress buried in the depths of the mountain ranges. It's been abandoned for what seems to be centuries. Could barely make out the outline of it on the feed.'

'All good points,' Griffin said. 'But doesn't prove anything.'

'He knows ... certain details. About the concept of a chimera virus. He knows things he shouldn't. We've had his claims independently verified. And none of it is looking good in the slightest.'

'In terms of the consequences? Or the fact that your informant knows stuff he shouldn't?'

'Both.'

'What is it? I've heard of a chimera virus before. I just don't know exactly—'

'It's an amalgamation of various viruses. Like the old mythological creature. Goat, lion, serpent — all combined. That's a chimera virus. They're trying to take the worst parts of a bunch of different shit and smash it all together into one super-virus — anthrax, smallpox, Ebola. I don't even want to think about what happens if they pull it off.'

'How close are they?'

'We don't know. The informant looked over a bunch of documents he wasn't supposed to have access to before he fled the monastery. But he got caught in the act. He barely made it out alive. So, even if they don't know that he's in our custody, they know he's out there somewhere. And they're probably hurrying this along. Or at least packing things up. They've had a week to get out of the monastery, but that's not going to be an easy task. We think they're still there.'

'Can you know for sure?'

'No. That's why we're turning to you.'

'I don't know what I can do. I'm not armed.'

'We can arrange certain things...'

'But why me?' Griffin demanded. 'I don't even know who you are. Round up the Bhutan military. Send in your own soldiers. Swarm the place. What can I do against a fourteen man paramilitary force? I'll get shot to pieces on sight.'

'Don't underestimate the amount of thought we've put into this. You're our best option. We've considered everything from dropping a MOAB on the monastery to sending all seven thousand men in the Bhutan army into the mountains to swarm the place. Everything we try and consider has a laundry list of disadvantages. You included.'

'But I'm your best shot?'

'Our informant tells us there's a giant subterranean cave complex underneath the fortress. That's why it took him so long to wise up to what was going on — he just thought he was protecting underworld VIPs.'

'Which means you can't storm the place, because you don't know where the caves lead.'

'Exactly.'

'And if they see you coming, they'll probably enact a contingency plan.'

'Yes.'

'And you can't bomb it, because the cave underneath it might not collapse the way you want it to, and then you'll lose the scientists forever after they escape.'

'Exactly. I knew we were looking at you for a reason.'

'So what is this?' Griffin said. 'You want me to run into an ancient fortress and take out fourteen men?'

'That's not including the scientists themselves. We want them all dead. If our informant's telling the truth — and all signs point to it — then these are some corrupt bastards. They're being paid to deliver a bioweapon into the hands of terrorists. So you need to take out the paramilitary force, and the creators themselves.'

'And you think I'd accept that? It's a death wish.'

'In fact, I know you'll accept it,' Lars said. 'I know almost everything about you. We don't recruit anyone here. We only accept the best of the best, and on top of that it takes a certain personality type to do what we do. You fit that personality type. You've acted selflessly in the field countless times, and we think you'd make a unique fit to Black Force. I was going to tell you all of this on March 15th, but we need to hurry along with the schedule.'

'So this is a job offer?'

'It is. And we're giving you the worst case scenario for your first operation before any of us have even met you. But your Operator Training Course results are something to behold. We think you haven't had enough experience in the field to realise your true talents. We think you might show that today. You don't know what you're capable of, but we do.'

'You're good at selling your services.'

'I have nothing to sell. It's just an offer.'

'And if I don't accept?'

'Then we're probably going to have a chimera virus in the hands of a volatile mercenary force. We don't know their motivations, or what they want to do with it. But our informant's telling us there's a general undercurrent of anti-American sentiment amongst all of them, so it's not looking good for our capital cities. That's why we're involved.'

'I'm your last resort?'

'More or less. We can try other things, but they'll almost certainly fail.'

'Fly in a convoy of Special Forces soldiers. Surround the area. Flush them out.'

'We're not amateurs, Colt,' Lars said. 'What makes you think we haven't already thought of that?'

'I just don't see how—'

'The fortress is in full view of the Paro Airport, which I'm sure you know happens to be one of the most dangerous civilian airfields in the world. There's less than a dozen civilian pilots who are allowed to land on that tarmac. And their fortress happens to have a direct line of sight to the airport. So we'd have to land somewhere else, and trek in on foot. It'd take weeks. And they'd see us coming from miles away. They picked the mother of all defences, whether they intended to or not.'

'So they'll see me coming.'

'That's the point. You're a nobody. You can get in close and then raise hell.'

'Like I said,' Griffin said. 'It sounds like a death sentence.'

'You sign up for Black Force, and you're signing your own death warrant. That's the nature of the beast. But you have the chance to do great things along the way. And that's all I can ever promise you. The rest is up to you.'

'I'm your best shot at pulling this off?'

'Yes. You are.'

'Then I guess I don't have a choice,' Griffin said, before common sense could tell him otherwise.

5

T he Dzong stood out amidst its surroundings — Griffin had passed the complex by many times before, but had never imagined he'd be striding inside its walls during his time in Bhutan.

A few days ago, a conversation with a pair of British tourists who had spent a month learning everything they could about the Paro Valley and its history had brought him up to speed on the country's architecture. He knew a Dzong consisted of a fortress-like structure surrounded by smaller administrative buildings, temples, and a high perimeter wall. He knew the Bhutanese military occupied a handful of these complexes in the Paro Valley.

Now, he strode straight up to the entrance of one of them and waited patiently for a pair of perimeter guards to meet him.

He couldn't believe what was happening. He'd absorbed Lars' instructions quietly and patiently, but what he was about to do seemed like some far-off, distant dream. The surreal nature of his surroundings didn't help — it was like he'd been transported back to medieval times, moving through a quiet cold valley with the concept of combat on his mind and rudimentary plans running through his head.

It didn't take long for the Bhutanese military to respond to his brazen arrival. Lars had reassured him of their co-operation, but once again none of it felt real.

The pair of hard-faced guards — Kalashnikov rifles swinging off straps on their shoulders — stormed up to him, anger lacing their expressions.

They studied him for a silent few seconds. If he hadn't been the man they were expecting, he wondered if they might have chased him off with their rifles raised.

But the call must have gone through, because one of them nodded once and ushered Griffin straight through into the complex.

A spiralling gravel trail twisted up to the main building, complete with vast stone walls and enormous wooden entrance doors constructed in an imposing fashion. A particularly cold gust of wind whipped through the complex, setting Griffin's nerves on edge. He was an imposter in this land, an alien presence who — for reasons the Bhutanese military couldn't possibly fathom — had been allowed to step foot in the complex and arm himself with an arsenal of weaponry.

Griffin didn't know the finer details. Lars had contacted the relevant parties and the urgency had clearly been stressed. Maybe it had gone directly through the President. Whatever the case, the Royal Bhutan Army occupying the Dzong had been told to hand over whatever Griffin needed, no questions asked, to deal with an undisclosed matter.

Nevertheless, Griffin wasn't about to go all out. He still needed to make the trek to the monastery itself, which would test the limits of his physical capabilities. He would need to pack light, and dual-wielding assault rifles would achieve nothing anyway.

He followed the two perimeter guards wordlessly up to the main fortress in the Dzong. They hadn't exchanged a shred of conversation, and Griffin imagined they didn't speak a word of English. He didn't speak a word of Dzongkha either, so he elected to stride patiently behind them and bow his head to protect himself from the sudden chill.

The calmness of his trip to Bhutan had dissipated the second he'd hung up the payphone. Now his senses were heightened, cortisol flooding his brain as he became wired, tuned into his surroundings, fully aware. He was about to step into a brutal world he hadn't anticipated visiting for at least a couple of weeks. That required a change in demeanour, an icy hardness that was already starting to settle over him.

The vast wooden entrance doors of the Dzong swung open to greet them as they reached the entrance. Griffin stepped through into a high-ceilinged foyer that had been converted into a military administrative room, complete with sprawling desks piled with documents and several more Bhutanese men spread out across the tiled floor. A couple had M16A2 assault rifles resting by their side, but there weren't many weapons in the room.

Griffin imagined the Royal Bhutan Army didn't run into terrorist threats all that often.

With a population of just over seven hundred thousand, the bad eggs were likely few and far between.

Actually, it seemed they were condensed into one geographical hotspot buried in the mountains of Great Himalaya.

One of the Bhutanese men — a thirty-something man

dressed in faded army fatigues — rose from his chair and crossed the enormous foyer, the sound of his footsteps echoing off the hardwood far above their heads. He drew to a halt only inches in front of Griffin and furrowed his brow.

'Weapons,' Griffin said, electing to keep things simple.

'You don't need to speak to me like a child. I'm the translator.'

'Oh.'

'I take it you're just as unwilling to share the purpose of your visit as my superiors were.'

'Afraid so. It's a matter of national security, though.'

'We do not need an American protecting us.'

'I never said you did.'

'Interesting...'

'Look,' Griffin said. 'I'm on a tight schedule here. Either give me what I need or send me on my way and deal with the consequences later.'

'Is that a threat?'

'I know almost as little as you do about all of this. Trust me. Just help me out here.'

'You don't need to beg. I have to help you out. Those are the orders. But don't think I'm happy about it.'

'I don't care what you think.'

With the tension crackling in the air, the translator led Griffin through to a converted windowless room deep in the bowels of the fortress. Metal shelving had been erected around the room, and a collection of weaponry rested atop the shelves. Griffin cast his eyes over a few Kalashnikovs, a Heckler & Koch G3, and an assortment of Browning sidearms. He stood in place, mulling over his next steps, Lars' words ringing in his ears.

'Well,' the translator said expectantly. 'Help yourself.'

'I'm just thinking.'

'I don't know what you need these for, but I hope your intentions are good.'

Griffin could sense the desperation in the man's tone. He wanted something, anything, to reassure him. Being kept in the dark was a horrifying experience under the correct circumstances — Griffin thought of the last couple of weeks of his life and understood exactly how the translator was feeling.

'My intentions are good,' he said. 'I'm sorry I can't say more.'

'Is your business in the Paro Valley?'

'I can't say.'

The translator didn't respond, but the tension considerably amplified. Griffin ignored the cold sweat materialising in his palms and crossed the tiny room. He picked up a black INSAS assault rifle — carted over from India, no doubt — and studied it. Truth was, he hadn't been this uncertain in his entire life. He had listened to every word Lars had said regarding the advised approach to the monastery, but he had never taken a risk like that before.

Leave the big guns, Lars had said. *Take a Browning Hi-Power and act like a lost traveller.*

But Griffin couldn't bring himself to do that. Striding up to an ancient fortress with a sidearm and a barebones plan of attack was asking to die.

He had to look at the situation objectively. Everything Lars had told him about the mountain temple all but eliminated a conventional approach. Trying to storm the fortress with guns blazing would best be reserved for the Royal Army, and it more than likely wouldn't work.

And there were few ways to conceal a full-auto assault rifle.

Griffin gulped back the humid air and put the INSAS back into place.

He picked up a loaded Browning Hi-Power, collected four additional fifteen-round magazines — giving him seventy-five total 9mm rounds to work with — and slotted the weapon into his waistband, drawing his belt tight over the gun.

Then he turned back to the translator.

'I'm done,' he said, wondering whether he was making the biggest mistake of his life.

6

T   he translator froze in place. Sweat had appeared on the man's brow. It was clear that he was nervous. Griffin couldn't imagine the extent of the man's uncertainty.

'I don't understand,' the translator said. 'I was under the impression you were preparing for war.'

'I just needed a gun. One gun. There must have been a breakdown in communication.'

'What are you doing?'

'We already discussed this. I can't—'

The speed with which the translator drew his weapon astonished Griffin — he missed the half-second window to wrench the Browning out of his waistband, and as a result found himself staring down the barrel of an identical sidearm.

Looking death in the eye.

There was nothing pleasant about having a weapon pointed at you. Griffin didn't take it lightly. Even though the translator was no doubt rabid for answers and uncomfortable with a stranger moving freely through his building, that didn't excuse the gun.

Griffin turned his face to stone. 'Put that down.'

'No!' the man barked. 'What is this shit? I get a call from my commander saying that I need to let an American arm himself, and that it's out of my hands. You will tell me what you are doing or—'

'Or what?' Griffin barked. 'You going to shoot me right here? Good luck explaining that.'

'You will not leave this room until—'

Griffin cut him off for the second time consecutively by raising his arms up in the air, palms facing the translator, who had taken up the entire doorway in an effort to look imposing. Griffin allowed as much innocence as possible to creep into his expression and he stepped forward with tentative motions, even though his heart hammered against his chest wall.

'Let's just calm things down,' he said. 'You don't want to get into this. I'll be out of your hair now. I just needed a Browning.'

'Why do you need the Browning?'

'You don't let up, do you?'

'I want to know. I'm not comfortable with letting a complete stranger walk out of this building armed. No matter what my superiors say.'

'You're a soldier. You follow orders. What do you think you'll achieve by disobeying your commander?'

'What if he's corrupt? What if you're going to go and kill innocent people? I could not live with myself.'

'I'm not going to do that.'

'How can I know for sure?'

'You're just going to have to take my word for it.'

'That's not good enough.' The translator reached down

with his free hand and yanked a bulky satellite phone out of the pocket of his fatigues. He tossed it underhanded across the room and Griffin caught it. 'I was told to give this to you. It's got GPS co-ordinates preset into it by whoever is responsible for you.'

'Did you look at the co-ordinates?'

'Of course.'

'Were you told not to?'

'Of course. Why are you headed into the mountains?'

'I'm not allowed to share anything with you,' Griffin said.

He took another step forward. The translator's grip tightened around the trigger of his weapon and for a moment Griffin froze up, convinced that his time on this planet was up because of a paranoid, trigger happy Royal Army soldier. But the Bhutanese man remained in place, and Griffin inched to within lunging distance of the translator.

'You going to put that thing down?' Griffin said.

'Not yet.'

No-one had come running in to defuse the situation, mostly because they were both still speaking in calm, controlled voices. But there was no mistaking the horrendous fear in the air — both from the translator trying to squeeze out answers, and from Griffin wondering whether the man would pull the trigger and everything would go dark.

He kept his demeanour as relaxed as possible, waiting for the slightest opening.

'Please tell me,' the translator said, growing increasingly frustrated. 'I want to know that I'm doing the right thing.'

'You are doing the right thing, but I've received direct orders not to—'

'Fuck the orders. Tell me right now. I could kill you here and we could bury you out the back — none of the men in this building would care. We could tell your superiors that we let you out into the valley and never saw you again...'

'That wouldn't be very nice.'

'I don't know whether you are a nice guy or not.'

'Are we going to go around in circles all day?'

'No. You will tell me what—'

'Okay,' Griffin said.

'What?'

'I said okay.'

'Okay, you'll tell me?'

'If you really want to know, then—'

Halfway through the sentence Griffin reached out a hand with his fingers splayed, trying his best to make it seem like he meant no harm. It was a lackadaisical gesture — as if he were inexperienced in the realm of combat and simply trying to wave off the Browning pointed at his head. He knew he wouldn't be able to actually brush the sidearm away, but he only needed to...

Now.

His fingers hovered a few inches away from the barrel of the Browning and Griffin suddenly transformed into a raging battering ram, injecting his movements with enough explosive energy to take complete control of the situation in a heartbeat. With his outstretched hand he smashed the gun off the centre-line, knocking the translator's wrist into the closest wall. Simultaneously he powered his other fist into the guy's chin, transferring enough kinetic energy to send the guy sprawling off his feet. A *crack* emanated from the man's jaw and Griffin followed up by kicking him in the side of the head hard enough to knock him unconscious.

A fistfight, especially involving someone of Griffin's abilities, was always a strange dynamic. Before the confrontation had unfolded there had been no energy whatsoever in Griffin's limbs. Then he'd flooded himself with rage and decimated the translator in a couple of strikes. Now that the man was stripped of his consciousness, Griffin's limbs slackened and he returned to his usual demeanour.

The life of the patient warrior.

Brutality, then nothingness.

He crouched down and snatched hold of the translator's fatigues, dragging the guy over the threshold and dumping his unresisting body in the equipment room. The man would come to in a few seconds but it would take him a couple of minutes to get his bearings.

That was all the time Griffin needed.

He shut the door behind him and double-checked the Browning Hi-Power was still slotted into place in his waistband. Satisfied, he hurried down the corridor and emerged back out into the main foyer as if nothing out of the ordinary had happened at all.

None of the other Bhutanese soldiers spoke English, so Griffin simply smiled and nodded, indicating he had all he'd come for.

A couple of them nodded back, and ushered him to the open entrance doors leading back out into the biting cold.

He was not their concern.

He offered a farewell smile and left the Dzong fortress behind. He adjusted the duffel bag on his shoulders and strode down the gravel trail, heading for the same rural road cutting along the bottom of the valley, twisting and weaving through farmland.

Far in the distance the mountain range beckoned.

Griffin quickened his pace, sensing the darkness behind him. Soon the semiconscious translator would be discovered and all hell would break loose, but by then Griffin would be lost in the wilderness, trekking through North Himalaya toward an unknown threat.

Despite everything, something told him this was what he had been put on this earth to do.

The timing was too coincidental. The ancient monastery drew him toward the mountains, and he simply put one foot in front of the other and followed.

Fourteen mercenaries.

He didn't stand a chance.

But he wouldn't have been able to live with himself if he'd refused. He would have turned on the television one day and heard about a chimera virus unleashed upon a nation, tearing innocent people apart from the inside.

No.

He now knew why he'd ended up in Bhutan.

The satellite phone in his hand beeped intermittently to correct his course, but for the most part the journey into the mountains consisted of Colt Griffin alone with his thoughts, putting one foot in front of the other without a sign of life in any direction.

He had ample opportunities to accept his potential fate. He'd seen combat before, but nothing of this nature. Nothing of a one-man-army variety, which apparently his life would become if he survived this ordeal and accepted a position in Black Force's ranks. The thought tantalised him, and the strange nature of the approaching combat actually sent a shiver of anticipation down his spine.

Time and time again he looked to his left, and then to his right, as if expecting to find fellow soldiers heading into the madness.

But it was just him, alone in the valley, draped in civilian clothes with a rucksack on his back and a semi-automatic pistol shoved into the waistband of his outdoor hiking pants.

A nomadic wanderer, headed for trouble.

It suited him fine.

Then all those thoughts melted away, replaced by an existential dread that permeated through to his core. He had to come to terms with the fact that he might die in these mountains, but it bothered him far less than he'd originally expected. He had taken each promotion during his career in stride, always keeping the knowledge in the back of his mind that every time he accelerated up through the ranks it carried a greater likelihood of dying.

He didn't care.

The flat stretch of farmland began to incline, beginning the ascent into the mountains. Griffin put his elite physical conditioning to work and ignored the lactic acid burning in his calves as he strode up vast hillsides. Every now and then he passed a local, all of whom shot him puzzled looks. They probably didn't see tourists this far off the beaten track without accompanying guides.

But he didn't need their concern.

He knew how to handle himself.

One hour blended into two. There was no going back — he had come too far. He fished into his duffel bag and took a long drink on a plastic bottle of distilled water, then wolfed down a pair of protein bars he'd picked up from a supply shop near the airport.

He'd figured at the time that relying on local food vendors could sometimes result in being stranded in the middle of nowhere without direct access to supplies, and now that precautionary measure was paying dividends.

He continued on, and the landscape became more alien still.

Griffin couldn't help but stare in awe at the staggering cliff faces all around him, most of the rock a mix between grey granite and stunning ochre. Lush vegetation covered great swathes of the cliffs, and there wasn't a soul in sight.

The sheer silence of the region struck a chord with him, making the Browning at his hip appear entirely unnecessary.

It seemed like an unsuppressed gunshot in these mountains would rival a blast of TNT in its intensity. It would disrupt the peace that seeped through the region.

But Griffin reminded himself that the peace had already been disturbed.

Despite the isolation and the wind howling through the mountains, the satellite phone never faltered. Connected to devices tens of thousands of miles skyward, it kept him on a straight path through the maze of rural trails, taking him up the side of cliff faces, always heading for the strange monastery tucked into the depths of the mountains.

Earlier into his trip Griffin had deliberated about visiting Tiger's Nest, the most famous monastery in Bhutan. Positioned in picturesque fashion atop a slab of stone on a mountainside, he'd decided not to venture that way at risk of having to mingle with a horde of tourists with similar intentions. He'd wanted to spend the trip finding peace with himself, heading far off the beaten track to destinations seldom visited by anyone.

Now, he was taking that concept to the extreme.

The GPS told him the ancient fortress was less than a mile from his current position, and his pulse quickened as he pressed forward along a zigzagging mountain trail running through the bottom of a narrow valley. Trees clogged the way on either side, and far above his head the cliffs and mountains speared into the sky.

He was an ant amongst titans.

Ten minutes later he made it out of the tree line, keeping

his hands looped around the straps of his duffel bag in case anyone was watching from afar. He had never imitated a foolish civilian before, and the experience proved strangely unnerving.

In linear combat, both parties were under no illusions as to each other's intentions. They simply wanted to kill each other.

Now, he was testing new concepts.

Deception.

Infiltration.

He whistled as he strolled, breaking free from the claustrophobic valley trail and stepping out onto a potholed road arcing up the side of a relatively steep hillside. That same hillside transformed into a staggering line of mountains, elevating into the low-hanging cloud and disappearing from sight.

And then he saw it.

Griffin narrowed his eyes and spotted the stone structure slapped into a narrow crook between two cliff faces — the building was enormous to be even visible from this distance, especially considering its state of disrepair. Moss covered the entire exterior of the fortress, to the point where Griffin's eyes might have passed over it had he not been specifically looking for it. It hadn't been preserved like the famous monasteries of Bhutan, instead left to rot away into the side of the mountain.

From this vantage point, Griffin recognised exactly what Lars had been talking about. There was no convenient approach to the fortress aside from strolling up to its entrance. The monastery was backed up against a sheer cliff-face, and the variable of a subterranean cave complex only complicated the issue.

Griffin could be walking into anything.

He had to accept that, and pray that the element of surprise would lean the odds in his favour.

Not a chance, a voice told him.

But he wouldn't do anything else.

He set off up the hillside before the rational portion of his brain could scream at him to retreat. One foot in front of the other — that was all it took. Before he knew what he was doing he'd set off in the direction of the fortress, and by that point there was no going back.

If the occupants hadn't seen him by now — a solitary figure powering up the largely empty hillside — then they deserved whatever they had coming their way.

But these were professionals.

And, sure enough, ten minutes into the trek Griffin looked up to see two foggy silhouettes descending down from the fortress complex. They were still at least a mile away, but everything was visible in this strange landscape, and it was inevitable that they would meet.

Griffin could do nothing but move to meet them. He discarded the satellite phone in a nearby bush and pressed on. He knew where the fortress was. Keeping the phone would only raise more questions.

The terrain turned inhospitable as he ascended out of the flat plains and dipped into the choking forests of the mountainside. Wind battered away at his shirt, and he reached up and wiped a thick lock of hair away from his eyes. He'd grown it out during his time in the Delta Force, and had been on the verge of shaving his head when his stint in Bhutan had taken a dark road.

This was the most stressful part. The approach. The awareness that whatever happened past this point would inevitably be violent. There was no alternative.

Thankfully, that suited Griffin just fine.

He looked up the trail and spotted the point in the mountainside where he would meet the approaching party.

And he spotted a window of opportunity.

He was unaccustomed to this. Combat, to him, was something straightforward. At least it had been in every circumstance so far during his career. Now he'd dipped his toe in the muddy water of something very close to espionage. This was not his life — he seemed like an imposter in his own skin.

But he would have to get used to it, because if he made it off the mountain his life would take a dark turn into deception.

The pair of paramilitary thugs approaching him didn't know who he was.

For the first time in his life, Colt Griffin sensed raw potential running through his system. He could act. He could play the fool.

And, as the two parties converged on the fog-laden mountainside, Griffin realised he was born to do this.

8

The thugs were taking no chances.

Griffin raised his arms as high as they would go, fingers splayed, and allowed an expression of unbridled terror to wash over his face as he pretended to notice the weapons in their hands for the first time. They both carried INSAS assault rifles, which set Griffin on edge. He couldn't imagine the men acquiring the weapons anywhere other than the equipment room of the Dzong he'd visited hours earlier. He envisioned one of the soldiers in the converted fortress nodding with greed as the paramilitary force flashed their cash.

Griffin had been right not to inherently trust them.

And it explained why the translator had been so jumpy.

If the man knew of the heavily-armed force in the mountains — and, in fact, had armed them himself — there could be little other explanation for Griffin's purpose. He'd probably been trying to avoid Griffin's arsenal being traced back to the Dzong.

Now, Griffin pulled to a halt on the churned dirt, steadying himself against the buffeting wind. At this altitude the cloud hung low and thick, blanketing everything in a weak fog. It gave the surrounding trees an ethereal look, as if Griffin had stepped into some kind of paranormal waste-land. The sound of his heart hammering in his chest didn't help the strangeness of the situation.

And it certainly didn't help that he would need to put on the acting performance of his life in a few short seconds.

'Whoa, whoa, whoa,' he shouted through the cool mountain air. 'What's up, guys? There's no need for any of that...'

Inwardly, he noted with bemusement that the pair of approaching hostiles were rednecks. Maybe Griffin had even grown up in the same town as them. They were both similar-looking, with close-cropped short brown hair and pudgy faces. They had the big, stocky builds of powerlifters, which Griffin had to admit took him by surprise. He couldn't imagine them carting gym equipment up to the monastery. He wondered how long they'd been stationed at the ancient fortress.

They held their weapons like untrained thugs, which they more than likely were. Ex-soldiers, no doubt, but there were varying degrees of military experience. Griffin imag-ined he was at the polar opposite end of the spectrum to the men in front of him. But that didn't change the fact that they were both armed with fully automatic rifles, and he was not.

That tilted things in their favour, unless...

'What the fuck are you doing out here, boy?' the man on the left spat, scorn in his voice.

'I-I'm sorry. I got lost. Am I not supposed to be here?'

'You're ten miles from the nearest town,' the guy on the right said. 'That's a long trek to make by mistake.'

For added effect he jabbed the barrel of the INSAS rifle in Griffin's direction. It would have been simple enough to catch the weapon at the very end of its jab and wrench it sideways and destroy the soft tissue of the man's throat with an elbow, but Griffin stayed in place. The guy on the left had a beat on him, and he couldn't eliminate two barrels pointed in his direction at the same time.

'Are you guys from the Royal Army?' Griffin said, even though it was perfectly clear that these men were more than likely from Texas.

But a foolish tourist would simply see the barrels of their weapons like a deer caught in headlights, and assume they were military of some kind.

The guy on the left grinned — sadistic in his glee. 'Yeah, boy. We're from the Army. In fact you're gonna have to come with us for trespassing.'

'Come on, guys,' Griffin said, faking a nervous smile. 'I'll turn around and be on my way, hey? No need to make this a scene.'

'Oh, I think you're too late for that, hombré,' the guy on the right said. 'You ain't supposed to be here.'

'Then I'll be off back down the mountain. Sorry to disturb—'

The guy on the left stepped forward and squashed the INSAS barrel into Griffin's throat.

Griffin froze up in apparent terror, trying his best to let the blood drain from his face. It helped that — acting or not — the risk of getting shot was high. It didn't matter how much training he had. These men were jumpy and clearly shocked by the appearance of a stranger at the foot of their base. He wondered how long it had been since they'd made contact with civilisation.

'Okay,' Griffin mumbled. 'Okay, okay. Do you want my money?'

'We've got enough of that,' the guy on the right smiled.

Griffin noticed them staring at each other, wordlessly deciding what to do with this strange bumbling tourist.

'We can't let him go,' the guy on the left said. 'He's seen us.'

'You think the boys downstairs will have any use for him?'

'I'm sure they will.'

'Let's hand him over then.'

Griffin knew exactly what they were talking about, but he had to pretend to be oblivious. His insides twisted as he contemplated the ramifications of failure — he would be handed over to the scientists in the subterranean caves, a human guinea pig delivered on a silver platter for testing purposes. It hardened his nerves — previously he'd been hesitant to dish out violence on these two men, considering how little he knew about them.

Now, though, he wouldn't hesitate.

The guy on the left circled around behind Griffin, dragging the cold barrel of his INSAS rifle along the skin of his neck. The metal caught on the side of his throat and drew a thin dollop of blood — Griffin felt the warmth running down to his collar. When the man had the assault rifle pressed against the back of Griffin's neck, he shoved him forward.

'Walk,' he said.

'Where are we going?'

'Just walk.'

'Could I please call my family and tell them—'

The guy shoved the barrel hard enough into the back of Griffin's neck to send him stumbling forward, almost taken off his feet by the force of the shove.

'Walk,' the man hissed.

The three-man procession meandered up the hillside,

heading further into the clouds. The guy on the right kept his rifle pointed at the ground, swinging it uselessly by his side with every stride. Griffin gave thanks for the man's ineptitude, but he probably thought his buddy had enough control over the situation to deem a second trained weapon unnecessary. He led the way, moving slightly ahead and a little to the right of Griffin. The other guy kept a measured pace directly behind him, never taking the INSAS barrel off the back of his neck.

Griffin scrutinised the path ahead — it twisted around a collection of rock formations jutting out of the mountainside. There were great sheets of granite slapped down at random across the uneven ground, proving large obstacles en route to the ancient fortress half a mile above.

Griffin could make out the outline of the monastery, but anything other than that was shrouded in a haze. Nevertheless he kept up the demeanour for as long as he was out in the open, just in case any of the men stationed at the fortress had eyes on them through the fog.

Then the trail crossed along the rear of a larger rock formation, blocking them from view of the monastery.

Griffin ducked away from the assault rifle's barrel as fast as his limbs would allow.

9

Take out the alert guy first.

Griffin had never experienced hand to hand combat at such a visceral level. His brief stints in the heat of combat had involved long range gunfire exchanges — not this. Not feet apart from a hostile who had every intention of shooting him down in the dirt, or beating him into a pulp. He'd been in street fights before, but nothing carried the weight or the savagery of what he was currently embroiled in.

One wrong move, and he would die.

It was oddly freeing. He found himself connected to his body, putting every last ounce of effort into every movement, aware that the failure to give it his all would result in a bullet in the back of his head.

So he threw his head off the centre line and jerked back, crashing into the guy behind him with all his bodyweight. Air exploded from the guy's lips as Griffin smashed into his stomach with all two hundred pounds of his frame. He bent at the knees and then burst upward, knocking the INSAS rifle skyward with his shoulder. Then he was at close range, so he gripped the guy's customised military fatigues, spun him around and hurled him into his comrade.

The pair went down, and Griffin was already on top of them.

He wrestled the INSAS rifle off the first guy, simply using brute strength to wrench it out of the man's grip. A gunshot this close to the monastery, amidst such silent surroundings, would spell nothing but disaster. Griffin knew he couldn't allow a round to be fired. So he spun the bulky assault rifle in his grip and swung it like a baseball bat down at the first guy's head.

He underestimated the power of adrenalin.

There was a sickening crunch and the man went limp. Griffin wasn't able to know for sure, but he expected the guy was dead — or very close to it. He turned to the other hostile — who had just managed to wriggle his way out from underneath his friend — and swung the rifle's stock with the same ferocity into the centre of his chest. Another crunch sounded, and the guy went down wheezing and spluttering, his own rifle forgotten.

Griffin kicked it away, then let fly with another swing of the rifle for good measure, targeting the same centre mass.

A third consecutive crunch rumbled down the mountainside.

Then there was silence.

Griffin let the quiet drape over the trail. He knew the limits the Operator Training Course had pushed him past, and he knew of the untapped physical potential that he'd never had the chance to use, but it hadn't become clear to him until that moment.

Lars' words rang in his ears.

We think you haven't had enough experience in the field to realise your true talents.

He stood there on the mountainside, recognising what lay in front of him but having trouble comprehending how it had happened.

It had all felt so incredibly ... easy.

The first guy was definitely dead. Griffin didn't spend long lingering on the sight of his corpse — one side of his skull had been caved in by the rifle swing. The other guy was silently wheezing, pale as a ghost, clutching his chest. His internal injuries were no doubt severe, but he would stay alive for a while longer. That said, he seemed incapable of speech. His eyes had almost rolled into the back of his head from the sheer amount of pain he was in.

Griffin couldn't conjure up any kind of remorse. These men had been ready to hand him over as a test subject for some kind of super virus. In fact, he thought the first man had got off easy by being subjugated to such a quick death.

Then again, he wasn't one to linger on suffering.

He set to work immediately, even though he didn't quite know the reasoning behind his actions. Lars had told him he would improvise in the moment, and he was obliging. He'd come to the mountain without the slightest hint of a plan, and as expected things were falling into place. Each action opened a new realm of opportunities, and he pounced on the first one he saw.

He spotted a woollen balaclava hanging out of the dead guy's combat belt — likely to protect from the cold at this altitude. Everything lined up. He set to work stripping the corpse of its clothing. In less than a minute he tore off his old civilian hiking clothes and slipped into the dead guy's faded military fatigues, likely picked out of the Bhutan Royal Army's surplus and stripped of any identifiable symbols. Then he switched his hiking boots for the mercenary's combat boots and tugged the balaclava over his head.

With one hand he snatched up the INSAS rifle he'd used to beat the two men into the dirt, and with the other he hauled the second guy to his feet.

The man winced and groaned and turned even paler still.

'Come on,' Griffin muttered. 'We've got work to do.'

He looped his free hand around the guy's back, supporting the man's weight. The guy wouldn't be able to stand on his own. The blows from the rifle might have shattered his sternum. He would have trouble breathing, moving, and speaking for quite some time.

That was, if he survived his injuries.

'You—' the guy started, and Griffin smashed the heel of his palm into the man's lower jaw.

He felt a couple of teeth dislodge under his hand and the guy drooped his head, spitting blood into the dirt.

Griffin steadied the guy's weight on his free arm and set off in the direction of the monastery.

He couldn't allow the man to speak a word when they entered the fortress.

That was, if his rudimentary attempt at entry even made it past the first stage.

10

A s soon as they emerged out from behind the rock formation, Griffin expected his head to be blown off by a long-range gunshot.

There were too many variables.

The three consecutive impacts with the rifle had broken bone after bone, and surely the reverberations must have echoed up the trail...

Surely Griffin had spent too long behind cover — masked from view of the fortress — to arouse suspicion...

Surely he looked nothing like the man he'd just beaten to death with a single swing...

Surely, this wouldn't work.

But Griffin had no more time to think, because the trail reached its natural conclusion at the base of the enormous staircase in front of the monastery. A set of stone steps spiralled up, culminating in a pair of massive entrance doors at least twice the size of the Dzong military building Griffin had been so awed by hours earlier. They hung invitingly ajar.

Griffin immersed himself in a second acting clinic and

bowed his head in apparent pain as he hurried his supposed comrade up the staircase.

The guy on Griffin's arm eked out a grunt of agony as he moved. He could barely keep his feet underneath him, even though Griffin was supporting most of his bodyweight. There was little chance he would be able to alert his comrades in the monastery that all was not as it seemed.

I hope.

He needed the guy on his arm to lend the scene any credibility whatsoever. Even identifying Griffin as an imposter would require a double take at the very minimum, and he simply needed those few beats of hesitation to make his move. Having one of the paramilitary soldiers hanging off his arm would make things more believable.

Perhaps not for long.

But Griffin didn't need long.

He confirmed the INSAS was ready to fire, because any kind of hesitation once he was within the walls would spell disaster. Satisfied, he screwed up his face in an attempt to signify immense pain — having the added effect of disguising his features through the wool of the balaclava — and hurried to the top of the staircase. There was no-one in sight, but once again he recalled Lars' words.

Fourteen men, not including the informant.

He'd dispatched two.

Which left twelve heavily armed, highly motivated hostiles to take care of.

Plus the scientists, whoever they were and wherever they were.

But the presence of the two mercenaries revealed one thing — the entire convoy hadn't fled yet. The chimera virus was somewhere in this monastery, or underneath it. That gave Griffin all the motivation he needed to make the near-suicidal move of striding straight through the gargantuan wooden doors and stepping into one of the grandest entranceways he'd ever laid eyes on.

He soaked in the sights in a heartbeat. It was similar in layout to the military-occupied Dzong, only three or four times larger. The ceiling was domed and soared far over Griffin's head. The walls and floors were made of smooth grey stone, and the rounded shape of the structure made it seem like the entire space was a monolithic antechamber to the mountain itself. Griffin thought of the cave complex beneath his feet and realised the fortress was exactly that.

More importantly, there were four or five men spread out across the largely-empty space, each of them dressed in similar unidentifiable khaki fatigues. A couple wore plain T-shirts above their khaki pants, revealing muscle-bound physiques.

Griffin figured it was an aspect of the job to appear imposing, especially when one's occupation involved providing paramilitary services to rogue scientists in the mountains of Bhutan.

So a fistfight simply wouldn't work — namely because everyone in the space was armed and seemingly prepared for combat. Despite that, they were spread out awkwardly, having adopted no particular formation or prepared for what strode through the doors.

'What the fuck?' one of the men cursed, speaking English with a thick European accent. 'What happened?'

'He was armed,' Griffin spat, thanking the heavens that the man he'd killed also hailed from Texas. It was effortless to impersonate the guy's accent, because Griffin shared it.

There was an awkward pause as the nearest man scruti-nised him — perhaps particular intonations in his tone hadn't added up with the man he'd killed. Then the guy shook it off and continued.

'Where is he?'

'Dead. He hit our man though.' Griffin nodded in the direction of the semiconscious guy he was carrying on one arm.

'*Our man?*' one of the mercenaries up the back said, his voice echoing across the cavernous space.

I don't know his goddamn name, Griffin thought.

He weighed the options and came up short regarding any believable way to proceed. The more he kept talking, the greater chances these men would have to pick up on the subtle cues and realise he wasn't who he was pretending to be.

'Take that fucking balaclava off,' another voice snarled. 'Why are you wearing it in the first place?'

Griffin couldn't do that, because then his long black hair would spill out and the jig would be up.

He'd hoped to worm his way into a more advantageous position before shit hit the fan, but it seemed like this was as good as he was going to get.

He dropped the guy on his arm to the stone floor, raised the INSAS rifle to his shoulder and let off the fastest burst of his life.

11

H e had the narrowest window of time with which to take advantage of the element of surprise, and he used it to the best of his abilities.

There were two men closest to him with bulky, fear-some-looking weapons in their hands, so Griffin simply turned to each of them and drilled a couple of rounds through their chests. They weren't wearing protective gear of any kind, probably assuming the confrontation with the single straggler didn't have a hope of reaching the monastery itself.

And that was why Griffin succeeded.

The tide turned at once — the remaining mercenaries stopped in their tracks as automatic gunfire roared into exis-tence, resonating off the surrounding walls. A couple had been in the process of instinctually moving toward Griffin and the injured hostile.

A natural reaction to seeing a wounded comrade.

But suddenly the comrade had begun to unload bullets in their general direction, which had no doubt overridden their motor functions and thrown them into combat mode at the drop of a hat. Griffin targeted one of the men — who was in the process of gathering his weapon off his shoulder strap — and fired a short three-round burst. Things were unfolding too fast to get a full picture of the damage he'd inflicted, but the guy dropped all the same. Blood sprayed, and the two men Griffin had shot first finished cascading to the floor.

Three down.

There was one guy left in the entranceway. Cortisol flooded Griffin's senses and he battled to control it — adrenalin threatened to overwhelm him. His insides constricted with such tension that for a moment he thought he might pass out from the sheer overload of sensations that came with a battle rush. But he kept his wits about him and wheeled to aim at the final man.

This guy was well over six feet tall.

A blessing in disguise, considering he was the furthest from the entrance.

And there was also the fact that he was raising his sidearm in Griffin's direction.

Griffin saw a muzzle flash, but that in itself proved the guy had missed. If the bullet had struck home he would have seen nothing except a sudden darkness, like a television being pulled out of the power switch. The blinding flash of light lit up his vision and the distant roar of a gunshot sounded a moment later, hitting Griffin's ears at the same time he fired a burst of his own.

Against a pistol, in a one-on-one duel, an INSAS rifle won almost every time.

The final man twisted and jerked as his torso was riddled with bullets from Griffin's rifle. He dropped too, less than a second after his three friends.

Barely any time at all had unfolded since chaos had broken out.

Griffin twisted on his heel, took aim, and sent a final unsuppressed round through the forehead of the man he'd carried into the fortress, putting the guy out of his misery. The guy had been in enough pain already, and Griffin felt no need to prolong his suffering.

But he couldn't stay still for a moment.

Despite the ringing in his ears — even though the fire-fight had taken place in a cavernous space, it had impaired his hearing all the same — soft distant outcries of surprise floated through the ancient temple. Griffin tried to make sense of where the voices were coming from, but too much was happening at once. He counted five corpses in the entranceway, added an extra tally mark for the man he'd beat down outside the monastery, and concluded that there were eight hostiles left to deal with if Lars' information was in any way accurate.

And he had no reason to doubt it.

But early success had nothing to do with what was to follow. The voices grew closer, seemingly echoing from everywhere at once, and Griffin realised if he didn't get the hell off open ground he would be shot down from any number of vantage points across the space.

He looked ahead and saw a grand staircase twisting up in two prongs to a landing overlooking the entire lobby. The enormous clay blocks composing the structure itself were whitewashed, but fading under the ravages of time. Nevertheless the integrity was sound, and as Griffin's hearing recovered he realised the voices were condensed into the space behind the landing.

There would be armed men on that landing in seconds.

He didn't doubt it.

He simply had to move.

He lowered the INSAS rifle off his shoulder and broke out into a sprint, leapfrogging a couple of the nearest corpses. He could barely hear the sound of his boots on the stone floor, drowned out by the sound of his heartbeat throbbing in his ears and the roaring of adrenalin clouding his senses in a foggy haze. Despite that he made it to the base of the two spiralling staircases in record time, spurred on by nerves. The neighbouring structures twisted around to a meeting point far above Griffin's head, converging on the landing in the shape of an hourglass.

Griffin chose the left-hand staircase at random and hurried up the stone steps, taking them three or four at a time.

At the top of the staircase a figure materialised.

Griffin's heart skipped a beat and he made to raise the rifle in the direction of the threat, but a single glance at the man above him revealed the guy hadn't quite put the scene together yet.

'You hurt?' the guy called down as Griffin thundered towards him.

Griffin realised he was still wearing the balaclava, and breathed a silent sigh of relief as he figured he'd carved out a narrow window with which to capitalise on the confusion.

'No,' he said, and fired two rounds through the guy's throat.

12

T he mercenary's limbs slackened just as Griffin reached the top of the staircase and burst out onto the landing.

He couldn't slow his momentum — and he didn't want to in any case — so he simply shouldered the now-dead man aside and wheeled on the spot, searching for any sign of nearby hostiles. He realised he'd spun in the wrong direction as soon as he sensed movement out of the corner of his eye, and for an instant he thought his time was up. He nearly closed his eyes in anticipation for the gunshot he knew would follow, but instead of a lead round punching through the side of his head he caught a moving body to the side of his torso, all the kinetic energy transferring across.

Someone had crash-tackled him.

As soon as he sensed the oncoming impact — as thunderous as it may be — he knew he could utilise the momentum to his own advantage. He dropped his hips half a foot lower as soon as the guy slammed into him, bending at the knees to lever the odds in his favour. When the impact happened, Griffin wrapped one hand around the hostile's waist and hurled the guy over the top of him.

A standard judo throw.

The guy spun over Griffin's lowered torso and slammed into the stone floor on the other side, limbs flailing in all directions. Griffin had executed the throw with precision but it took him off his feet all the same — in the carnage, he wasn't able to maintain a hold of his rifle. It sandwiched awkwardly between himself and the guy he was coming down on top of, and both of them jolted in fright as the weapon went off between them.

The bullet went wide, slicing out from between the brawl, and both of them burst into action as soon as they realised they were unharmed. Griffin lost all awareness of where the gun had ended up — somewhere underneath him, no doubt — but any attempt to make a snatch for it would leave him vulnerable, exposed to a punch to the back of the head. In a situation like this, where testosterone crackled in the air and nervous energy reached a fever pitch, he knew it would only take one strike to put him out of the equation for good.

So instead of making a snatch for the rifle he secured an advantageous position on top of the newly materialised combatant and crashed a fist into the underside of the guy's jaw.

Now that he had a window in time with which to gather his thoughts, he took a look at the guy underneath him. The man was Caucasian, somewhere in his thirties, with one hell of a mean mug and deep-seated wrinkles etched into his forehead. His eyes were cold and soulless, a characteristic Griffin imagined was required in the kind of field the man operated in.

Up close and personal, it was the first opportunity

Griffin had to study one of the mercenaries. The rest of the altercation had been an endless blur of blood and steel.

He studied how his punch thundered into the man's throat and came away satisfied with the result. Inadvertently, he took a moment to compose himself and load up for another devastating punch, which he considered a potential fight-ending blow.

He swung back a fist, arching it high into the air, ready to bring it down on the soft tissue of the guy's neck and hinder him for long enough to fetch the INSAS rifle and finish the job.

Then that all fell apart.

As he reared up on his haunches, he made the amateur mistake of putting enough distance between himself and his opponent for the guy to throw a desperate strike. After all, Griffin had considerably little experience in situations like these. He was making it all up as he went along. Training could only take you so far.

So when he swung his fist back, the mercenary underneath him came up with a picture-perfect elbow, putting his heart and soul into the blow. Griffin had been hit countless times before in training, but any kind of controlled sparring had some level of restraint that needed to be showed. Even in a street fight, no-one was looking to kill the other party. Here, in this ancient fortress buried in the mountains of Bhutan, it was life or death.

Which injected the elbow thrown in Griffin's direction with enough force to cause serious damage if it connected.

It did.

Griffin felt a sickening *thwack* against the side of his head, and his own punch fell apart. He'd cocked his arm right back in preparation to bring it down with thunderous

ferocity, but now a switch snapped in his brain and his arms
and legs turned to jelly.

Fuck.

He was fully conscious. Fully aware of his surroundings.
But something had rattled inside his skull, and it seemed as
if he'd turned horrifically drunk for a few vital seconds.

Panicking, Griffin tumbled off the mercenary and staggered to his feet, putting as much space between himself
and danger as he could during the vital seconds it would
take to recover.

If he couldn't regain his composure in the next few
moments, he would certainly die.

Terror leeched through him as he stumbled across the
landing like a drugged lunatic.

13

E yes wide, brain reeling, Colt Griffin clawed for survival.

He had never experienced this before. A couple of times on the sparring mats, during his years of extensive combat training, a stray shot had slipped through his guard and accidentally knocked him unconscious. It was part of the job description. Flash knockouts were uncommon, but they happened if you put enough hours into training at maximum capacity. But they involved a sudden departure from the realm of consciousness, an overwhelming darkness that shut the lights out in an instant.

This was different.

It was cerebral, and raw, and terrifying.

He'd been "rocked", a term he was all too familiar with, save for having any true first-hand experience with the sensation. Now he understood it all at once. He tried to plant his foot on the stone floor to stabilise himself and it lurched uncontrollably to one side, the knee buckling as Griffin tried to stay on his feet. He reached out with the other foot and it behaved in similar fashion. For a wild moment he lurched across the landing with the gait of a newborn giraffe. There was no time to think about how ridiculous he looked. He sensed a surge of movement behind him and realised the mercenary was closing in, charging after Griffin in an attempt to capitalise on his hindered state.

Griffin didn't bother looking back. Any attempt to put up a fight would be disastrous, considering that he could barely keep his feet underneath him. His brain swam, clouding his vision and throwing his equilibrium off. Nausea crept up his insides as he struggled to return to full awareness.

Still, the mercenary closed in.

Griffin sensed the man right behind him and knew another crash-tackle was inevitable. He was in no shape to execute another judo throw, let alone put up any kind of resistance. He accepted the fact that he would be taken off his feet within a couple of seconds...

...and then he put his foot down and it held.

There was barely anything behind the motion, but it supercharged him with a newfound confidence. It was like snatching onto a handhold right before he was set to tumble off a cliff. He established the slightest amount of balance and sucked in a deep breath of air, throwing caution to the wind.

He would get one attempt at a strike.

Still mentally foggy, he wheeled on the spot and launched a high kick with as much technique and power as he could muster given the circumstances. The toe of his combat boot darted through the air, and Griffin was moving so fast that he barely had time to check whether he'd aimed for the right location. He'd simply thrown it with reckless abandon, aware that if it didn't connect it would throw him off his feet and leave him at the mercy of a furious, blood-thirsty paramilitary thug.

But it connected.

Griffin didn't see the impact — he only heard the brutal *thud* of his boot slamming against someone's jaw. The kick connected with such ferocity that it sent his leg hurtling back in the other direction, ricocheting off the guy's face with a *bang* similar to a gunshot. Griffin knew he'd broken bones in the man's face, which was often enough to end the fight right then and there.

For good measure, Griffin sized up the portion of the landing where the thug had come to a crashing, frozen halt and hurled himself across the space. He clotheslined the guy across the chest, slamming an arm against his sternum with two hundred pounds of bodyweight behind it.

The guy lurched back into the ancient railing...

...and toppled over the edge of the landing.

A long second passed before the *crunch* from far below echoed off the walls. Griffin didn't even bother looking down to check whether the man was dead, or simply gravely injured. Frankly, he didn't have time. It might have been merciful to try and put the guy out of his misery but Griffin couldn't hold onto thoughts like that for any longer than necessary. He was still out on wide open ground, surrounded by an unknown floor plan, with — if his estimations were right — six hostiles still unaccounted for.

And that didn't take into consideration the horde of scientists somewhere below the monastery, whoever they were and however many of them there were. Sure, they might not have combat experience, but Griffin didn't take anything lightly. A man with a purpose and a shot of adrenalin to the veins could do all kinds of wonders. And if the chimera virus was as sinister as Lars' rudimentary explanation had indicated, then even one scientist escaping through the cave complex would prove disastrous.

Because then the survivor — or survivors — would be out there in Bhutan, having witnessed the murder of their comrades and having watched their plans fall to pieces. Griffin couldn't imagine the kind of rage that could build in the aftermath of that. He had already mown down eight of their men — a feat that would have astonished him had he taken the time to stop and actually consider it — and right now the remaining procession might be in sheer survival mode, hoarding as much of the chimera virus as they could before Griffin burst onto the scene.

Because they might not know that he was just one man...

These thoughts raced through Griffin's head, and he started to try and grapple with them when he heard a cacophony of shouts ringing through the upper level of the fortress. He wheeled on the spot, searching for the source of the noise, but found nothing.

You need to move.

Now.

The voice ushered him forward, and he obliged. Complete awareness had yet to return to him — he'd managed to deal with the charging mercenary, but his thoughts were still spaced out, his vision groggy and unfocused.

Reality came to him in jolting fragments.

Pale and sweating and gulping the thin mountain air down, Griffin staggered into one of the connecting corridors leading away from the open landing area. There were at least six different directions to head, so he chose one at random and set off like a drunk.

At which point all his inexperience and ineptitude caught up to him.

14

Griffin staggered down a stone corridor and plunged into pitch darkness.

He froze on the spot, suddenly cold, unsure whether the freezing sensation running down his spine was due to an actual change in temperature or simply an amalgamation of the injuries he'd received.

It's the concussion, the voice of common sense whispered in his ear.

He knew it was, but he didn't want to accept it. He'd been beaten to hell during the Operator Training Course — and during all the training he'd undertaken in the United States military before that — but nothing had altered his state quite like the elbow that had plunged into the side of his head. He couldn't think straight, see straight, hear straight. The kick he'd managed to land on the mercenary's chin had effectively been a stroke of luck, because now he could barely walk in a straight line without his vision lurching from one side of the dark stone hallway to the other.

A severe concussion no doubt stripped most of one's

motor functions away, and Griffin found himself surprised
that he was still conscious. When the elbow had connected
it felt like his entire head had exploded. Perhaps in any
other situation it would have shut the lights out, but he had
some primal understanding that if he blacked out at any
point over his time in the monastery, he would certainly die.

Maybe his brain was holding on for dear life.

It certainly felt like it.

At the same time, years of combat training had been
thrown out the window. It took him a solid twenty feet of
stumbling before he realised he hadn't even picked up a
weapon on his way off the landing. There'd been a couple to
choose from, discarded by various hostiles, but he'd simply
heard the approaching voices, recognised his hindered state,
and fled.

He reached for the Browning Hi-Power in his waistband,
a last resort...

...and found nothing.

It had come loose during the fight, discarded somewhere
on the landing or across the monastery floor below.

He couldn't believe it.

He was unarmed.

The complete lack of natural or artificial light didn't
help to calm him down. He seemed to recall — through the
hazy fog of his memory — that the cavernous entranceway
had been illuminated by floodlights across the perimeter
walls. It made sense, considering this monastery had seemingly been abandoned for years. To set up shop, the mercenary force had lit up the portions of the fortress that they
needed to occupy.

This corridor, evidently, was not one of them.

When he figured he'd plunged far enough into the darkness to make himself invisible, Griffin reared to a halt in the

middle of the stone floor and dropped to his rear. It hurt, but he couldn't bare to stand a moment longer. Close to hyper-ventilating, he bowed his chin to his chest and stared at the floor, even though he couldn't see what lay a foot in front of his face.

Panic set in.

He couldn't help himself. Applying for the Delta Force had been a gruelling and rigorous process, ordinarily reserved for only the best soldiers in the U.S. military. Griffin had always considered himself up to the standard.

But this was fucked.

There was no other way to describe it. He had killed — or beat half to death — eight men in the space of a couple of minutes, and during the last portion he'd received one of the more severe concussions possible. Now he was barely able to string a cohesive thought together, alone in a freezing dark corridor deep within a monastery he knew nothing about. For all he knew his efforts would be in vain and he would find himself lost in the darkness, with no way out of the maze until he succumbed to dehydration or mere insanity.

He tried not to dwell on those thoughts. They did him no favours. In fact he knew he was exaggerating, for he turned and looked over his shoulder to see the dull glow of the upper level landing far in the distance. Amidst the soft light emanating off the far walls, he saw shapes twisting and writhing.

Silhouettes, moving about the landing, assessing the scene.

More mercenaries.

Griffin doubted he could go much further. He hadn't even bothered to reach down and scoop up one of the weapons in the heat of the moment — clearly his mental state was diminished. How did he expect to put up any kind of fight against the men that were left?

Because you made it this far.

He took a deep breath, supercharging his brain with fresh air, and sensed some of his spatial awareness returning. He'd studied the concept of proprioception during his military training — the awareness of one's body in space. That had been dismantled by the elbow, but it was now returning.

Griffin got his feet underneath him and levered silently upright.

He had nothing to do but slink toward the source of the conflict and do his best to cause as much damage as he could.

He couldn't see a way out of this situation alive. Even if he dealt with the six men in front of him, one of the scientists would probably escape with the valuable cargo intact. Griffin had spent too long in the monastery already. The alarm had been raised. They were probably packing their gear now, ready to flee into the subterranean depths.

But all that didn't stop him from putting one foot in front of the other.

So he crept forward.

And suddenly found himself taken off his feet by a jarring impact from behind.

It had come from deep in the darkness...

15

A t first he thought he'd been shot, considering the severity of the jolt. He sprawled face-first into the stone floor, bringing his hands up to prevent his nose breaking against the ground. But then he recognised the impact as blunt force trauma...

...and heard the muffled '*oomph*' of a surprised combatant falling alongside Griffin.

Someone just ran into me.

It was the only thought he needed amidst the tumultuous series of events.

The man had run into Griffin from behind, heading for the landing in a flat-out sprint. Griffin hadn't heard him approaching because of the effects of the concussion, and the guy hadn't sensed Griffin in front of him until it was far too late. He evidently hadn't expected this section of the fortress to be populated.

Neither had Griffin.

As soon as Griffin realised the man had come down alongside him, he intuitively shot a hand out through the darkness and clamped it down over the guy's mouth, crushing the unseen hostile's cheeks between his fingers in an attempt to stop him from crying out for help. The guy writhed under Griffin's grip, but Griffin held tight with the strength of someone who knew he was clutching at survival.

Griffin contorted the rest of his body, scrabbling across the cold stone to try and get a better position in the darkness. He couldn't see, and his vision still swum, but his accuracy and timing were beginning to return. He kept his palm pressed down over the guy's lips — who had started trying to bite Griffin's fingers off — and reached down to wrap an arm around the guy's throat.

Griffin was a black belt in Brazilian jiu-jitsu, something that had taken him thousands of hours to achieve with no visible signs that he had achieved it. It was a strange phenomenon, and something he had thought long and hard about. There were men and women walking out in society who could strangle you to death in a thirty-second window, but no-one would ever know it. Jiu-jitsu didn't rely on strength or brute force — rather, it was about technique and leverage. Strength certainly helped, which was why Griffin found it effortless to slip his arm around the guy's neck and torque the choke hold with all his might.

Strength was the difference between choking someone unconscious in ten seconds, or twenty.

And in this ancient fortress, every second counted.

But as soon as Griffin secured the choke he found himself being lifted off the ground as if he weighed nothing. He blanched as he realised the man he was trying to kill was a giant. The guy was pushing seven feet tall, and looping one arm around his neck was like trying to strangle a tree trunk. Griffin hadn't been able to tell in the dark, but now he found himself hurled off the stone floor, suspended in space, hanging off the guy with one arm looped around his neck and the other clamped over his mouth.

And everything was still pitch dark.

The guy jerked and shimmied and twisted on the spot, aiming to hurl Griffin into one of the stone walls and smash all the breath from his lungs. Griffin transitioned into a guillotine choke in one fluid motion, swinging around the giant's frame and blindly adjusting the hold on his neck. Now he hung from the guy's neck like a front-facing backpack, his legs looped around the man's stomach and his elbow pressing down on the base of the neck with relentless pressure.

It didn't take long.

The big man managed one muffled grunt of protest before the pain became too much as his head folded toward his chest under the boa-like squeeze of Griffin's bicep. The guy's legs gave out from underneath him, and on the way down he tried to slam Griffin down on his back with enough ferocity to cause permanent injury.

Thankfully, Griffin had been bracing for it, as it was basically the only way the man was going to survive the guillotine choke.

He took the impact in the small of his back, aware of the likelihood of being paralysed but unwilling to give up the guillotine choke. It was his one shot at staying in the fight. If he released it the man would scream out and his comrades would come running.

Five on one in a dark hallway could go no other way.

But the man's chin stayed compressed into his chest and the blood was no doubt rushing to his face as he battled with the immense pain. Griffin kept all his weight on the top of the guy's head, even amplifying the power of the choke when both of them sprawled onto the concrete floor. The slam had been the giant's last-ditch effort to get out of the hold, and now that the pain was mounting even further his will to win was sapping away. Griffin felt him accept the choke and sink into unconsciousness.

Then Griffin kept squeezing.

He barely gave it a second thought. He had already killed eight men — what was a ninth going to change? During the Operator Training Course, he'd grappled with the morality of killing unprotesting combatants, especially in the heat of the moment. How could he live with himself if he made the wrong decision, especially due to the morally grey nature of combat?

But none of that even weighed on his mind in the present moment. Everyone in this monastery had one intention in being here — protecting a group of paid-off scientists conducting experiments that mashed together a variety of different bioweapons into one super-virus. There was no doubt about their morality.

Griffin continued squeezing until he could no longer feel his arm, certain he'd caused enough damage to kill the guy. Perhaps it made it easier to enact in the darkness — it removed an element of reality from the situation. He clambered off the corpse and searched the ground around the body with his hands. Either his mind had been playing tricks on him, or he'd heard the metal clatter of a gun hitting the floor when the man had run into him.

Sure enough, his fingers clasped around the grip of a semi-automatic pistol.

It was pitch dark still, and Griffin couldn't discern the exact make or model.

As he ghosted back in the direction of the landing, he realised it didn't matter either way.

He had a gun, and he'd eliminated more than half of the

mercenary force within a couple of minutes of forcing his way into the monastery.

We think you haven't had enough experience in the field to realise your true talents.

Lars had been right.

Five to go, Griffin thought.

He had thrown himself into this world of life-or-death combat with such tenacity that he suddenly understood perfectly how men became addicted to fighting for their lives. If he didn't succeed in this fortress, there would be countless deaths at an indeterminate point in the future. That could be tomorrow, or a week from now, or a month, but eventually Griffin would hear reports of a chimera virus being unleashed in a populated area, tearing through civilians like they were nothing.

So, for the first time since he'd stepped foot in the monastery, Griffin felt some semblance of calm.

For the first time since he'd got the call from Lars, he felt in control.

He crouched low and stalked through the darkness, weapon in hand.

Now he was the hunter.

16

There were five left.

That was the only thought occupying Griffin's mind. His vision shrank to a tunnel, and it had nothing to do with his surroundings. As he drew closer to the light of the landing and the soft glow began to amplify, he looked down and recognised the weapon as a BUL Cherokee, native to Israel. There seemed to be little consistency across the mercenary force's arsenal, which led Griffin to believe the operation had been rushed — they must have utilised their combined resources and snatched up as much firepower as they could get their hands on in a narrow window of time.

The fact that he was even connecting those dots meant his critical thinking was returning.

It was hard to discern just where his mind was at in the darkness. He'd been grasping onto consciousness moments earlier, and with this level of sensory deprivation it was hard not to lurch from one moment to the next without stopping to consider his mental state.

But he seemed focused again.

Maybe the concussion would have long-term effects. It was still there, buried in the back of his mind, but the immediate consequences had dissipated. Griffin surged forward, staying as quiet as he could. Muffled voices floated from the landing, trickling down each of the connecting hallways. As he came to within twenty feet of the broad entranceway to his corridor, he paused in the shadows and listened intently for any sign of opportunity.

Finally, the odds had shifted in his favour.

He heard general panic in the air. On top of that, amidst the barbed insults being thrown back and forth across the landing, he sensed the frustration of the language barrier. These men had been mixed and matched from a variety of different paramilitary organisations, it seemed.

More evidence of a rushed job.

Griffin wondered what kind of opportunities the scientists were trying to capitalise on.

He wondered what they were being paid to carry out the experiments...

General commotion unfolded and Griffin heard footsteps shuffling on stone. Sharp commands were barked — a couple of them in English. Griffin paused in the shadows and smacked the side of his head as quietly as he could. The more debilitating effects of the concussion were fading, but the rest of it was still there. The blurred vision, swimming from side to side. The hearing loss. Everything sounded muffled.

He couldn't focus on anything for more than a few seconds.

He opted to stay in a crouch by the side of the corridor for as long as he needed, realising that foolishly charging out into open ground would only result in a quick death. The voices dissipated, and Griffin realised that the surviving men were disappearing into the bowels of the fortress, heading down any number of the darkened corridors.

Retreating?

He couldn't know for sure.

But there was still motion, coming from somewhere ahead. Griffin dropped to a pronated position and slunk on his belly over the stone. A strange sensation settled over him as he crawled — the floor underneath him suddenly became more real, more palpable. It was like he'd been coasting through a dream sequence for the last few minutes of his life. Now things were getting serious as his senses returned. Reality set in. His consciousness was restricted, and he was still no closer to dealing with the threat. He could take out mercenaries for days on end, and it would mean nothing if the scientists underground escaped with their payload intact.

So he pressed forward, sensing every scuff and dent in the smooth stone. He came out into the light and surveyed the scene — sure enough, there was still one man breathing on the landing. He'd been left behind to take care of the bodies — or he was simply distracting himself with a task instead of standing motionless as a sentry, unwilling to be alone with his thoughts.

For the first time, Griffin sensed genuine fear in one of his adversaries.

The man was Caucasian, with close-cropped blonde hair and the slender frame of a long-distance runner. His combat fatigues hung loose over his physique, but there was athleticism there. Griffin sensed dexterity and true combat ability. The guy moved with practiced poise, dragging his dead friends over to the banister to clear space on the landing. Griffin didn't know why the man was doing it. It made zero tactical sense. But there was the possibility that he had been close to the mercenaries Griffin had killed, and wanted to do something with their bodies other than leave them where they lay. The rest of the party had submerged themselves back into the monastery's corridors, no doubt to search for the intruder, so this guy had put himself to work.

Griffin felt a momentary stab of pity.

Then he remembered why he was here, and all that fell away.

He waited until the Caucasian guy had turned his back on the darkened corridor, and then surged out into open ground like a wraith released from hell.

The guy never even saw him coming.

Either he was inexperienced in true combat, or the death of his friends had ruined his ability to think straight.

Whatever the case, Griffin opted not to blow the back of his skull open with the Cherokee, because that would alert everyone in the monastery that he was still near the landing.

Instead he leapt the final couple of feet and crash-tackled the blonde mercenary into the stone floor like a football player flattening a wide receiver.

The guy had been using one hand to drag his dead comrades across the landing, and in the other he'd clutched an identical BUL Cherokee — the mercenary force must have got a batch of them from a supplier, off the books. Now that same Cherokee went flying as the man got hit by the equivalent of a freight train. Griffin deduced that no-one else was in the immediate vicinity and temporarily dropped his own weapon to deliver a thunderous elbow into the guy's forehead as the pair of them came down on the stone floor.

He snatched his Cherokee back up and jammed the barrel into the bridge of the guy's nose, leaning enough pressure on the weapon to cause the man horrendous pain.

'Speak English?' Griffin hissed.

A half-second of silence unfolded before Griffin raised the barrel of the Cherokee a couple of inches off the guy's nose and smashed it down, destroying the guy's septum. The man made to let out a howl of agony but Griffin clamped a hand over his mouth, cutting off the outcry.

'I'll keep doing that until your nose is mush,' he said, his voice barely above a whisper. 'Now answer my questions without hesitating, and if you tell one lie I'll squeeze this trigger. Speak English?'

'Y-yes,' the guy muttered, blood pouring from both his nostrils and leaking into his mouth. 'I'm American. For God's sake.'

'Where from?'

'New York.'

'How'd you get into this business?'

'Uh...'

Griffin simply raised the barrel of the weapon off the guy's nose and he went white as a sheet, aware of the kind of power Griffin could deliver from a single stab of the metal cylinder. He held up both hands in protest. 'Sorry, sorry. I got dishonourably discharged. Needed work.'

'You needed work?'

'Yeah...'

'Who's paying the scientists?'

'What?'

'Don't play dumb. I know what you're protecting. Down there. Underground. Who's paying them to make the chimera virus?'

'If I tell you the truth, will you let me go?'

'I think it's best to think about what will happen if you *don't* tell the truth.'

'Fine. You asked. They're the ones paying us, you dumb fuck.'

'The scientists?'

'Who do you think's bankrolling this thing? We're mercenaries. You think we'd be doing this if we had two brain cells to rub together? We follow the money.'

'Who are they?'

'The boys in the kitchen?'

'If that's what you want to call them.'

'Bunch of undesirables. I guess that's what you'd call them from your high horse.'

'I wouldn't get into a discussion about morality from your position,' Griffin said.

'Gotta get paid.'

'That's your reasoning?'

'Spare me,' the guy spat. 'You know how many tens of millions of people die every year? Who gives a shit if I help a few along that path? Just trying to make something of myself.'

'You trying to redeem yourself before I kill you?'

'Nah. Do what you gotta do.'

'The chimera virus. What is it?'

'The substance itself?' the man said.

Griffin nodded.

'How the hell am I supposed to know? I'm not a scientist.'

'You've been around it, I assume. How long have you been here?'

The mercenary had built up some confidence during the back and forth. He held his tongue just long enough for Griffin to turn irate. Before the man could squeeze out any information, Griffin smashed the Cherokee into the guy's already-broken nose.

This time, he did howl, and Griffin couldn't clamp his lips shut in time.

But there was no-one around to hear.

'How long have you been here?'

'About six months.'

'And how far along is the virus?'

'I told you—'

'Don't play dumb. You know something. Anything. Better start sharing it.'

'Alright, alright,' the guy said. 'Look — you want to make a deal?'

'Want me to hit you again?'

'I'm serious. I know a lot. I'll tell you all of it, but promise to kill me afterwards.'

Griffin paused, the barrel of the Cherokee hovering ominously over the guy's shattered septum. His face had become a mask of blood. Ordinarily Griffin would have found the sight grotesque, but that concept hadn't even passed through his mind yet. He saw nothing but a man holding back information about a super-virus. He would do whatever it took to get that information out.

Even if it meant causing irreparable damage.

'You really want to die?'

'Yes,' the man said, with an intensity that made Griffin hesitate.

He hadn't noticed yet, but tears had been forming in the guy's eyes.

No, not a guy.

A kid.

Griffin stared down at this kid — only a couple of years younger than him but all over the place mentally — and understood where he was coming from. The man had been submerged in a path with a one-way ticket to riches, and it seemed he'd had been moving so fast down that path that he'd never had time to consider the ramifications of his actions. Now that there was a gun pressed into his face, beating him to a pulp, he was starting to realise what he'd done.

Strange things happened to men who had never faced adversity in their lives.

This guy underneath Griffin was crumbling.

Physically, and emotionally.

Tears streamed down the kid's face now, mixing with the blood coming out of his nose.

'What have I done?' he whispered in the empty monastery, and in those four syllables Griffin sensed all the pain and realisation of a man whose entire moral core had shattered.

Now the kid was trying to pick up the pieces.

Griffin squashed the barrel of the Cherokee into his forehead. 'Talk.'

18

'It's a pathogen,' the kid mumbled. 'That's all I know. They're doing something with plasmids. They're not supposed to discuss it with the rest of us, but spend a month holed up in a place like this and people get talking eventually.'

'Plasmids?' Griffin said.

'They're inserting them into a pathogen. Like a virus on steroids. Combining a bunch of different stuff.'

'What stuff?'

'I honestly don't know. None of it's good.'

'Why are they doing this? What's their reason?'

The kid managed a wry smile through a mask of tears and blood. 'What's the reason anyone does anything?'

'What do they have to gain by wiping out a populated area? How's that benefit them in any way?'

'You really don't know...'

'I'm new to all this,' Griffin admitted. 'This life is wild. I don't understand it.'

'The scientists gain nothing from that. They don't care

about ideologies. But they can sell their product to people who do.'

'That's the end goal? Give it to the highest bidder?'

'There's extremists out there who will do anything to get their hands on this kind of shit. And some of them have billions. You know there's trillionaires out there? No-one believes it, but I've seen it with my own eyes. Everyone thinks these tech tycoons are the richest people on earth, but they have no idea. That's just the stuff on record. Most of this world operates outside of those parameters. That's who the scientists are selling to. That's how they never even have to think about money again...'

Now the kid's eyes were alive — he was consumed by the desire for cash. It had brought him into the mountains of Bhutan, and it had driven him to an existential crisis when he realised no amount of money could remove a piece of lead from your brain and bring you back from the dead.

'Do they have a buyer?' Griffin said.

The kid grinned.

Griffin smashed him in the nose with the Cherokee.

More blood sprayed.

The kid howled.

'*Do they have a buyer?*'

'Yes,' the kid said. 'And everything's already in place. Why do you think I've spent so long talking to you? They're already out of here. You've lost.'

Griffin's heart sank. He'd bought into the false hope that the mercenary underneath him had been ready to reveal crucial information about the "boys in the kitchen" down below. Now he realised he was crouched over a delusional child, a guy who no doubt expected to be provided with a lifetime of riches in exchange for delaying the intruder for long enough for the scientists to escape.

The kid saw Griffin realise this. His smile grew broader, exposing blood-coated teeth.

'If you were going to kill me,' he said, 'you would have done it by now.'

'That's where you're wrong,' Griffin said, and shot him through the top of the head.

19

There was nothing to do but select one of the corridors at random and sprint down it as fast as his limbs would allow.

He opted to keep the Cherokee and snatch up as many spare magazines as he could off the floor. Fetching an INSAS rifle would both slow him down and prove cumbersome in the tight hallways.

Griffin decided to follow the light. Each stone corridor had varying degrees of illumination, and he figured the brightest passage would lead to the most populated area. From there he could dispatch the four remaining mercenaries and figure out a way to reach the cave complex far below.

It pained him to realise that even though he'd achieved massive success over the initial portion of this mission, he was no closer to achieving his goal. In fact, every second that passed gave the scientists another moment to escape. Lars had mentioned that the subterranean complex could lead anywhere, and Griffin assumed the lab had been set up below ground to provide many avenues of escape if necessary.

So, in all likelihood, he had failed. He'd already been in the monastery for close to ten minutes, and the time he was now spending sprinting through a shadowy stone corridor signalled the chances of success leeching away. Lars hadn't wanted an all-out assault on the fortress because of this exact reason — it wouldn't take long for the scientists to realise what was happening and flee with the cargo.

He picked up speed, heart pounding in his ears, aware of the problem with this approach.

It was a lose-lose scenario.

The faster he moved, the greater chance he had of catching the scientists in their tracks. But that left them — plus the four mercenaries — ample opportunity to capitalise on Griffin's tactical mistakes. If he slowed down, he could approach with caution, but in all likelihood he would find an empty cave waiting for him.

So he pushed himself even faster.

He'd made it this far already. He had to trust his gut and press forward, even if it meant his own death.

The corridor seemed to constrict in size, and suddenly Griffin found himself hurrying through a long tunnel barely high enough to stand up straight in. At the same time the light dissipated — bulbs had been fixed into the walls at random, but they fell away as Griffin pressed further into the mountain. At any point he expected to run straight into a dead end and feel the claustrophobia begin to set in, but suddenly the corridor opened out into some kind of strange antechamber.

A circular stone room, devoid of any furniture or decorations of any kind, leading through into a larger room cast in darkness.

Griffin couldn't imagine anything lay further inside the mountain, especially not on this upper level of the fortress. He squinted, narrowing his eyes to try and make out the outline of what lay ahead. Then he noticed a dark hole in the floor of the antechamber room, and he darted his gaze in that direction.

There was a staircase.

Leading down.

And, as far as he could tell, a faint trickle of light crept up from the pit.

From far below.

Griffin had no time to consider the consequences. He aimed the Cherokee at the open space in case the fatigue that had set into his bones masked his ability to detect hostiles. His ears were roaring, no thanks to an elevated heart rate, and he wouldn't be able to discern if someone was lying in wait until he was right on top of them.

By then it would be too late.

He circled around to the top of the staircase, giant slabs of stone descending into darkness, and took a deep breath before setting off.

He put his combat boot down on the first step.

An explosion of noise and light and fried nerve endings washed over him — it took him a moment to realise he'd been shot in the foot.

He jerked his leg back before it gave out, going down a second later. His combat boot slipped on the puddle of blood already pouring out of the toe, but he didn't even put it together that it was his own blood. He thought he'd gone down on water, considering he'd lost all sensation in his foot and hadn't quite pieced together the concept of being shot yet.

Then the pain started to settle over him in nauseating fashion...

...but that was all stripped away by another deafening unsuppressed gunshot, coming up from below. The bullet must have passed over his head because he felt the displaced air beating down on him. It mustn't have missed by much either. The hostile at the bottom of the staircase had been targeting Griffin's centre mass in a space he'd been occupying a moment ago. Now he was spread-eagled on the floor, in disbelief at the overwhelming barrage of sensations, about to catch a bullet for his troubles when the remaining mercenaries found him laid out on the stone floor during one of the muzzle flashes that lit up the antechamber.

Griffin raised the BUL Cherokee, formed a rough estimation of where he'd last seen the shots come from, and fired three rounds in a tight cluster.

There was no return fire.

Griffin didn't even have time to gather his senses. He couldn't. He'd never experienced adversity like this — having to compartmentalise the knowledge that he'd been shot. He couldn't look down and discern how bad the damage was. He couldn't even make sure whether he'd killed the guy at the bottom of the stairs. The same thought from earlier washed over him.

His life had become a flow state of chaos.

He picked himself up, ignoring the stabs of agony coursing through his right foot, and set off hobbling down the staircase toward impending disaster.

There was nothing else he could do.

20

I f Griffin had considered the monastery's interior cavernous, he had nothing to prepare himself for the gigantic space he descended into as he reached the bottom of the staircase.

It was as if a prehistoric being had bent down, scooped a giant portion of the earth out, and resealed the ground back up again. The cavern was lit by enormous floodlights running along the natural ledges of the space, but even those artificial beams seemed minuscule in comparison to the sheer size of the underground lair.

Griffin had never seen anything like it.

From the outside, no-one would have suspected the mountain contained such an enormous natural space within. The entire cavern was shaped like a giant egg — Griffin had burst out onto a thin ledge about halfway up one of the rock walls. Most of the space was unusable, simply consisting of a web of ledges spiralling up toward the ceiling. But the floor of the cavern ran relatively flat, and Griffin stared down at least a hundred feet below to see an outburst of activity. Men — who from this height, looked like ants —

flitted back and forth between crude workstations, shoving apparatus into bags and destroying vital evidence. A couple of them had already begun high-tailing it toward a network of tunnel entrances against the far wall of the cavern.

Griffin gulped back apprehension. He counted four men total, none of them dressed in military attire. If he didn't know the background information he might have been completely lost observing the scene before him, considering the fact that no-one on the ground looked anything like scientists. Griffin didn't know what he'd been expecting. The mental image of men in white lab coats almost amused him — this wasn't a movie.

It was very, very real.

And that hit him when he tried to take a step forward and his leg gave out, collapsing on itself as the nerve endings in his foot jolted in agony. He grimaced, righted himself, and stumbled past the dead man at the foot of the staircase, who he could now see had caught a round through the upper chest. He was bleeding all over the rock shelf, but Griffin could barely make out the sight in the near-darkness. The floodlights tore through the space, arcing up toward the ceiling, but the cavern was so enormous that most of it lay shrouded in shadow regardless.

Griffin spotted the ledge spiralling down the cavern wall toward the floor.

He set off in that direction, ignoring the nausea tearing through him.

A shot rang out, causing everyone in the cavern to flinch. The unsuppressed gunshot resonated off the walls, echoing around the space. Griffin barely heard it though, because a shower of rock shards sprayed over him. The bullet had gouged a divot out of the wall right by his head. He ducked low but didn't freeze up — by this point he was so accustomed to forward motion that even a near-death experience couldn't slow him down.

A wet *squelch* sounded on the rock ledge underneath him and he glanced down to see a trail of blood following him down the ledge. The crimson stuff poured out of his boot — one look at the injury confirmed it was worse than he expected. He stared straight back up at the path ahead and resolved not to pay any attention to the bullet wound until his work was complete. The longer he spent focusing on it, the greater his chances of freezing in his tracks and collapsing in shock.

And that couldn't happen, because two of the scientists far below him successfully reached the mouth of the tunnel complex and disappeared into its depths, falling out of the floodlights' reach.

They vanished from sight.

Griffin pushed himself faster. He had to catch them...

It took a few minutes to descend to the cavern floor, and Griffin sensed his health deteriorating with each step. He didn't want to consider how much blood he'd lost from his foot, but he knew it was bad. He tried not to focus on it, but it was hard to ignore the swimming vision and freezing chill that descended over him as he made it to ground level and burst out into open ground.

His condition had worsened to such an extent that he didn't even consider where the hell the other three mercenaries had disappeared to.

By the time he reattached himself to reality and wheeled in a circle, bracing himself for an attack, it was already too late.

They fell on him in a pack — which surprised Griffin, as it would have been rather effortless to step back and blast his brains out as soon as he reached the cavern floor. They had tucked themselves in a tight unit into the shadowy space underneath the natural ramp he'd just descended. They were all armed — Griffin noticed the flash of steel as they tackled him to the floor — which made him wonder why they hadn't killed him already.

Someone tore the Cherokee from his hands and the grip of a pistol came scything out of the air toward his face. Before he could raise a hand to protect himself it crunched against the bridge of his nose, eerily similar to the punishment he'd dished out on the blonde mercenary upstairs.

The sound and sensation of breaking bone rang through his head.

He gasped for relief, in a world of pain. Someone crashed a fist into his stomach and he spat blood over the dusty stone, already bleeding profusely from both nostrils.

The cold barrel of the same pistol pressed into the side of his head, crushing against the soft skin above his ear.

'How many more of you are there?' one of the three snarled.

Griffin could barely see straight, but he craned his neck to spot a couple of the scientists hovering by the entrance to the tunnels, observing the proceedings with cold, calculated gazes.

'Go!' one of the mercenaries roared. 'Don't risk it. Get out of here. We'll rendezvous later. Take the mountain trail.'

The remaining pair nodded and fled into the darkness.

Just like that, all the scientists had vanished.

Griffin had failed.

21

'How many?!' the second mercenary yelled.

Griffin couldn't even make out their faces. All the floodlights were pointed at the cavern's ceiling, which cast a murky shadow over the cavern floor itself. He sensed an amalgamation of lab equipment and workstations dotted across the floor, but all the bulbs usually illuminating the scientists' work surfaces had been either smashed or switched off. It didn't help that the injuries were beginning to accumulate, and he'd entered what felt like a drug-induced haze.

'Eight more,' Griffin muttered, as if terrified to divulge the truth. He tried his best to act like a man who had been backed into a corner and forced to co-operate. 'They're coming down now.'

None of the three mercenaries could hide their fear. They cast each other dark glares, alternating between looking at their surroundings and staring straight up at the hole in the wall a hundred feet above.

'You'd better let me go,' Griffin said. 'Or they'll kill you.'

'I don't think so, buddy.'

The third mercenary — the biggest of the three, who hadn't said a word so far — hauled Griffin off the ground and pressed his semi-automatic pistol to the side of his head. The guy wheeled Griffin around to face the rock ledge, treating him as a human shield in case any reinforcements decided to show up and take a potshot.

Griffin muttered something inaudible.

'What?' the third guy hissed.

The other two mercenaries backed off — Griffin imagined their guns were trained on the space far above, anticipating an imminent firefight.

Griffin croaked, 'I said…', and then trailed off.

The mercenary tightened his grip around Griffin's throat. 'Spit it out.'

'You should check your six.'

The guy imperceptibly glanced over his shoulder. Of course, there was nothing there, and there were no reinforcements on the way, but none of them knew that. Griffin jerked his head away from the mercenary's BUL Cherokee pistol and reached up with both hands, moving lightning fast, aware that his life was on the line. He seized the guy's wrist and wrenched him off-balance. The mercenary stumbled a step and Griffin dropped him with a perfectly placed left high kick, probably breaking his jaw in the process.

The mercenary hit the stone, and before he'd even come to rest Griffin had the man's Cherokee in his own grip.

The other two had started to react, but not fast enough. By the time they had their weapons — both fully automatic Kalashnikovs — Griffin had fired two shots.

The first shot tore straight through the forehead of the guy on the left.

The second missed.

Griffin dove into a wild tumble-roll as the second guy let

loose with a hail of gunfire, so loud in the cavern that a newcomer would have imagined an impending apocalypse.

Thwack.

Strange... being shot didn't feel like Griffin had expected.

He'd always anticipated a crippling, debilitating wave of imminent agony.

But this was ... somehow even more terrifying.

Mid-dive, his right shoulder jerked back unnaturally and he spun out of control, tumbling head over heels and finally ducking behind one of the giant steel workstations erected in the centre of the cavern floor. An entire laboratory had been set up, and Griffin pressed himself down below the line of sight as a wave of gunfire followed. A strange disconnect set in, separating him from what he considered real — the same sensation he'd experienced back in the monastery. This was somehow worse, though. A strange numbness set into his shoulder, and the blood flowing down his arm didn't become apparent until it trickled through his fingers.

Then he noticed it, and looked over to find his right arm covered in blood.

He didn't even know where he'd been hit.

There were more pressing issues to worry about right now.

The gunfire ceased and Griffin stood up from his crouched position behind the workstation. In hindsight it was one of the most ridiculous tactical mistakes he could have possibly imagined, but the same effects were washing over him, obscuring his common sense.

This wasn't a concussion, though ... this was blood loss.

And it would be the death of him before long.

He saw the last remaining mercenary frozen out in the

open, searching for another magazine with a perplexed expression on his face.

Then Griffin realised that the man in front of him had made the exact same ludicrous tactical mistakes. All-out combat often stripped the best of their sensibilities, and this man was not the best. The guy had watched all thirteen of his comrades die grisly deaths in a state of disbelief, and now he'd foolishly emptied his weapon in the wild hope of finishing off this terrifying intruder. Now he stood in open ground, flabbergasted at how the tide had changed, searching his belt for a fresh magazine.

Griffin shot him three times in the chest before he had a hope of reloading his Kalashnikov.

And then there was complete silence.

Griffin stood rigid for a moment, gazing out over all he'd accomplished. Fourteen trained combatants lay dead before him. Even if he'd been at optimal health, it wouldn't have seemed real. Right now, with waves of nausea and chills running over him, the entire ordeal drew parallels to an extended dream sequence.

Griffin knew he would drop dead if he stopped moving.

So, even though he'd done more than he considered humanly possible over the course of his time in Bhutan, he turned on his heel and jogged straight into the network of tunnels.

He had a convoy of scientists to catch.

22

I t didn't take long to work out that — if he didn't receive medical attention — he had a finite amount of time left on this planet.

'You're in bad shape, Colt,' he muttered to himself as he staggered through endless tunnels with no end in sight. 'Real bad shape.'

He didn't know where he was headed, or what he would do when he got there. The long stretches of stone passages seemed to blur together into a continuous stream of confusion. Griffin wasn't sure he'd have been able to work it out even at one hundred percent capacity.

Now, though, he was running on ten percent.

A number that dwindled with each passing second.

Nine percent.

Eight percent.

Seven...

He couldn't see a thing. Every now and then he passed a dim LED cylinder fixed into the wall in a half-hearted attempt to light the way. But these tunnels were clearly unimportant to the scientists — albeit for an escape plan —

so they'd opted to prepare minimal lighting on their trek out of the mountain. Perhaps they'd already plotted and memorised a route through the tunnels, which would allow them to know exactly where they were headed in the event they needed to flee.

After ten minutes, Griffin began to work out that he had no hope of catching them. They had every advantage one could possibly imagine — they knew the terrain, they weren't injured, they had nothing to bear to slow them down...

Unless...

He recalled what the blonde mercenary had told him.

They're the ones paying us.

These weren't money-hungry scientists with no allegiance to anyone in particular. They were self-motivated, self-funded bioterrorists who had employed an army of fourteen paramilitary soldiers to protect them while they slaved away at a chimera virus deep underground. They weren't ordinary, run-of-the-mill bad guys. They had purpose in their actions. Intent in everything they did. If they had successfully created a pathogen, they would do anything to protect it.

Including giving their lives.

Griffin couldn't imagine they would allow their concoction to be placed in jeopardy. He posited what he would do if he was in their position.

Send all four of them running for the hills with a shred of a plan?

Or trust one man with the payload, and use the other three to hold back and ensure...?

He hadn't even completed that thought when he rounded a shadowy corner of the tunnel complex and the crowbar hit him full in the face.

23

There had been little noise — certainly nothing like a gunshot — but it had sounded like that inside Griffin's skull. He let out a moan as he crashed to the tunnel floor, whiplashing the back of his head against the ground as he fell. There had been nothing to dilute the force of the impact, and an ear-splitting headache roared into life behind his eyeballs as he rolled desperately out of the way of a follow-up shot.

Even though he had trouble staying conscious, he realised he could see the tunnel walls around him...

He caught a distant glimpse of an opening in the side of the mountain — daylight spilled through and flooded down the tunnel.

He was so close to the exit...

But the three men descended on him like a rabid pack of wolves, exactly as he'd imagined they would.

Of course they did.

They were highly motivated, experts of their craft. He should never have doubted them. They didn't have combat ability or weapons training of any kind, but they had determination, and sometimes that was enough. They possessed the initiative and the courage to independently create an underground laboratory and set to work going where no scientist had ever gone before. They were brilliant minds, and brilliant minds didn't always possess a moral compass.

These thoughts rang through Colt Griffin's head as they beat him down in the tunnel, the outside air so close he could taste it, the end goal within such close proximity yet so far away at the same time...

He had failed. The BUL Cherokee was nowhere to be found, knocked down the tunnel when he'd been taken off his feet by the initial crowbar attack.

Then, something clicked in his mind. Kicks and punches rained down on him, and the crowbar smashed into the small of his back, but above that some kind of ancient understanding took hold. He was not a particularly religious man, and he wasn't sure whether it was the proximity to death's door releasing strange hormones into his mind or some kind of deeper connection, but suddenly everything became clear to him.

This pain didn't matter.

He was still conscious, and if it didn't kill him he could walk through it for a minute or so.

Then he would collapse.

But only then.

So he surged to his feet amidst the barrage of attacks and thundered a fist into the jaw of the closest scientist, shutting the guy's lights out with a single strike. He dropped like a rag doll and Griffin stepped over his unconscious body to smash a front kick into the solar plexus of the second guy, driving him back into the stone wall. The guy bounced off the wall and Griffin floored him with a colossal head-butt, smashing the hardest portion of his forehead into the guy's nose. With two men hitting the deck, enough space opened up to wind up for a final strike on the third guy.

The one with the crowbar.

Griffin saw the steel whistling through the air toward him, but now momentum had transferred over to his side. He sidestepped the wild swing and beat the guy's face in with three well-placed punches to the forehead, nose, and jaw. Teetering on his feet, the man refused to go down, simply swaying on the spot and bleeding profusely from every orifice.

Big mistake.

Griffin stepped back, twisted a full revolution on the spot to build up momentum, and leapt into a side kick that struck the guy's throat with the equivalent force of a base-ball bat. Shin connected against soft tissue and the guy went down in a bloody heap.

Probably dead.

Griffin didn't have time to even consider what he'd done, or what kind of state he was in. He couldn't find the Chero-kee, but there was no time to search for it. There was one guy left, and Griffin had become possessed.

He spotted the narrow window of light far in the distance, and surged toward it.

One final man...

And he was the most important target of all.

Because he had the chimera.

And the keys to armageddon.

24

I t seemed ridiculous to Griffin that all the savagery he'd put himself through over the course of this operation all came down to a single duffel bag.

He burst out into the open, daylight flooding over him, only a half-minute after dealing with the three scientists who had elected to stay behind. He knew one man remained, even though it was highly possible that there was a separate convoy of scientists and all his efforts had been in vain.

But he knew.

Deep down, in his core, he knew this was the final hurdle.

It had to be. He couldn't go on any longer. As soon as he stepped out onto the thin rocky ledge facing out over the Paro Valley, he looked down to properly get a sense of his injuries.

Blood still pumped out of the toe of his boot, and the wound on his shoulder had started to hurt in a way he didn't consider possible — a deep, guttural sensation that tore through him and threatened to cripple him on the spot. On top of that the accumulated beating he'd absorbed was beginning to set in, dragging his limbs down as if they were moving through quicksand. He stifled a moan of agony and took his attention away from his broken body, looking out over one of the more picturesque views he'd ever seen.

This side of the mountain faced a luscious valley of vibrant green, dipping down away from the mountain range like a giant bathtub. Griffin had emerged roughly halfway up the mountainside, and a couple of steps forward would send him over the edge of a precipitous drop to the valley floor hundreds of feet below. The forest at the base of the mountain ran for several miles in every direction before giving way to scenic farmland for as far as the eye could see, only transforming into mountain ranges on the other side of the valley dozens of miles away.

'Beautiful,' Griffin muttered.

He caught movement out of the corner of his eye. Unsteady on his feet, he shuffled forward and peered over the ledge. Sure enough, this was not the only exit point for the tunnel complex. Below him were two separate holes in the side of the mountain, maybe a dozen feet underneath the ledge he stood on. A wild zigzagging combination of rock ledges and shelves arced away down the mountain, a natural trail leading to the base of the cliff.

Griffin began positing a way down to the forest floor when he spotted the last scientist on the ledge below him.

He couldn't help but think that fate had aligned them both. The natural slope of the mountain resulted in Griffin having a perfect view of the top of the guy's head. Their paths would intersect — albeit a dozen feet apart on the mountainside — in just a few short seconds. The guy hadn't seen him. He was sprinting along the narrow ledge, heading for the natural slope of the cliff in order to reach the forest floor as fast as possible. His feet were only a few inches from the side of the ledge.

It was a straight drop all the way down the face of the mountain if he slipped.

Griffin sized up the window, and came away unsure as to whether he would make it or not. In his mind, it was fifty-fifty. An overcommitment would send him sprawling off the side of the mountain, and holding back would result in landing on the uneven ground, losing his footing, and spilling off the side of the ledge regardless.

All or nothing.

He didn't have time to think. He spotted the thick black duffel bag swinging off the man's shoulder. It was stuffed full of something, zipped up and secured. It contained everything he'd entered this monastery for, and if the man got away with it, everything Griffin had done would have been for nothing.

His final thought before he jumped was of the chimera.

The mythical beast. Part lion, part serpent, part goat. An amalgamation of creatures, just as the virus was an amalgamation of the worst components of the world's deadliest pathogens.

He couldn't begin to imagine how much damage it could cause.

He realised, in a single moment of clarity, that his entire life had been a chimera. A fusion of different circumstances that had ultimately put him here, on this freezing mountain ledge with a collection of grievous injuries, gifting him this opportunity to put his life on the line to stop a greater threat.

He still wasn't sure if he believed in fate.

He took a deep breath, waited for the last scientist to run directly underneath him, and jumped.

25

It was further than he anticipated.

He wasn't going to make it.

Fuck.

The scientist noticed the giant silhouette bearing down on him from above and flinched involuntarily, ducking away from the incoming object at the last moment. At the same time Griffin landed awkwardly on the upper portion of the slope itself, leaving him with nothing to steady his fall. The steep angle of the mountain sent one of his ankles twisting gruesomely to the side, and with a sharp crack the bone shattered. He didn't notice it because he spilled forward, tumbling and lurching onto the lower ledge itself.

He'd made it.

But momentum was not on his side.

The way in which he'd landed sent him careening forward head-first, with no handholds in sight to slow him down. He was going to go over the edge of the mountain. There was no alternative.

Except...

As he was falling he reached out and snatched hold of

the duffel bag, managing to catch the very edge of the material in two fingers. Employing a pincer-like grip, he held on for dear life as the rest of him spilled over the side of the ledge. The duffel began to slide off the scientist's shoulder and the man visibly panicked, snatching and clawing at the bag that contained his magnum opus.

Although Griffin was battling for mere survival, rabidly trying to find balance on the ledge's precipice, he stared straight into the scientist's eyes. It unnerved him how normal the man looked — he was a white man in his thirties with thinning brown hair and a slightly crooked nose. Other than that he was unassuming — on a residential street, Griffin would have considered him an ordinary law-abiding family man.

But the eyes revealed all, and in those eyes Griffin saw darkness and cruelty and malice. He knew then, without a doubt, that the man in front of him would do anything to protect the contents of his duffel.

Griffin tugged backward.

The bag slid further off the guy's shoulder. It was simultaneously Griffin's lifeline and the object that would send the scientist spilling over the edge if he held onto it. Griffin had both feet scraping the edge of the cliff and the rest of his body suspended in space, propped up by the duffel. He was heavier than the scientist, and the man stumbled forward a half-step, unable to prevent himself being dragged off the ledge.

The scientist realised his predicament.

If he held onto the bag, Griffin's raw strength would send both of them tumbling off the side of the mountain. If he let go, it would save his own life but send his most cherished work cascading away to the forest floor. He would never find the bag in time.

The man had a choice to make.

And Griffin could do nothing but hold on for dear life.

In truth, he hadn't quite considered the ramifications of the situation he found himself in. It didn't exactly click that he had no way out of this mess. His focus had been captured so entirely by the sinister contents of the duffel bag that he had ignored his own safety.

He tugged again.

His survival instinct had disappeared. He wasn't sure if his injuries — and the severe concussion he'd suffered inside the monastery — had stripped him of his sensibilities, or if subconsciously he understood that nothing was more important than getting this chimera virus out of the hands of the man who intended to sell it.

Whatever the case, he didn't put it all together until the scientist's face contorted with a furious acceptance...

...and the man let go of the bag.

Griffin hung frozen in the air for the briefest of moments.

Then he clutched the duffel bag to his chest and tumbled off the mountainside.

26

He couldn't have fallen for more than ten seconds, but it gave him all the time in the world to think.

He thought of choices. He'd thrown a dart at a map and it had landed on Bhutan. He never would have done that had he been kept in the Delta Force after his Operator Training Course, and he never would have ended up here, completing a task for the division he'd been forced out of the traditional military structure to join.

Fate.

He might believe in it after all.

He thought of the directions lives could take. He'd seen brilliance in the eyes of the man on the ledge, and he imagined there was brilliance in his own eyes too. He never would have considered it possible to do what he'd just done, and he realised he was so content with death because he had never anticipated making it off the mountain alive. He'd accepted his own demise the moment he got the call from Lars Crawford, which made it all the more satisfying that he'd managed to complete the task along the way.

He didn't know what was in the bag he clutched against

his chest. He fell back-first toward the forest floor, staring up at the mountainside as it shrank rapidly from his view, and for a brief moment he thought he saw the awed face of the man he'd wrenched the duffel bag off, leaning over the ledge to get a look at the intruder who had torn his dreams away.

Colt Griffin fell, and as he fell he squeezed the bag tighter. He'd never know its exact contents. All he knew was that he'd prevented something awful, and he would take that satisfaction to the grave. He would never know who the scientists had intended to sell the chimera virus to, or whether they'd even succeeded in creating the super-virus at all.

But the look on the last scientist's face had revealed the truth.

They must have succeeded in creating the chimera.

Because Griffin had never seen someone so distraught.

He carried that mental image with him, searing it into his brain, imprinting it on his subconscious.

He had succeeded.

And the men in the monastery had failed.

All eighteen of them.

Now I know what I'm capable of.

Then he hit the ground and all his thoughts ceased forever.

27

Three days later, Lars Crawford woke to the sound of his landline phone shrilling in its cradle. He shook his head groggily from side to side, taking a moment to realise where he was. Truth was, he hadn't slept much over the past few nights. The uncertainty, the sheer unknown of it all, had been eating him alive.

He suspected this call would clear up most of what he'd been wondering.

He slipped out of the otherwise-empty double bed and padded across the room to his desk. There was no view to gaze out over as he lifted the receiver to his ear. His bedroom was a dull box, courtesy of what little time he spent at home.

His entire life was work.

And sometimes, like right now, work seeped into his core.

'We found the body,' the voice at the other end of the line said, and even though Lars had been anticipating those exact words he still sunk his head in despair.

'What happened?'

'He fell off the mountain.'

'Fell? You're sure?'

'I doubt he committed suicide. He landed on his back. His internal organs were pulverised. But we found a black bag clutched to his chest with enough spores of a bioweapon inside it to destroy an entire country.'

'Jesus Christ. How close were they?'

'They weren't close... they'd done it. We're looking at the samples in the lab, but it's worse than anything we've ever seen before. They mashed an entire chain of pathogens together — if it got released into the atmosphere and found hosts, it would have spread like nothing we've ever seen before. Maybe even worldwide.'

'What were they planning to do with it?'

'It's an ongoing investigation.'

'You said you recovered three bodies of men from Zenith Laboratories who went MIA?'

'Correct.'

'I'm led to believe there are four missing.'

'We're on his tail.'

'The last guy?'

'Yes.'

'Who is he?'

'Ben Ware. Nothing notable about him whatsoever, apart from his scientific capabilities, of course. An ordinary family man before he set off on this crusade. I'll never understand how minds work, Lars. The world's gone mad.'

'By "on his tail", you mean...?'

'We know his rough whereabouts. He's good at creating monster viruses, but he's not an expert at covering his tracks.'

'I have operatives who can take care of him.'

'I don't doubt you anymore, my friend. You sure know how to select them. What the hell is this scene we found? Seventeen dead. Seventeen. Colt Griffin didn't even work for you yet, for God's sake.'

'There's a limit to what our training can do,' Lars said. 'Some people just have it in them. It's my job to find them, and use them to the best of their abilities. Griffin had it in him.'

'Imagine he had training. Imagine what he could've done.'

'There's no point imagining. He's dead. It's our job to find more.'

'You think he knew what he'd achieved before he died?'

'It sounds like he took the bag to his grave. Maybe he jumped of his own accord. Knowing he needed to carry the chimera virus to his death.'

'Why didn't he just throw it off the mountain?'

'I don't know. We'll never know. But he prevented a catastrophe. And I don't use that word lightly. I spend my entire life around this kind of thing. And what he stopped ... I can't imagine how bad it could have been.'

'We can't honour him. We can't hold a public funeral. No-one will ever know what he did.'

'That's what he signed up for. That's what they all sign up for.'

'Different breed,' the voice on the other end of the line noted.

'They certainly are.'

'You okay? You seem quieter than usual.'

'Just thinking.'

'It wasn't your fault.'

'I know. I did the right thing. But sometimes ... I just wonder if he knew what he was getting himself into.'

'He accepted the job, didn't he?'

'Through a phone call. Maybe he wasn't thinking straight. Maybe it all hit him when he got there, and by then it was too late to turn back...'

'Does it matter? If he didn't accept your offer, he never would have been able to live with himself.'

'I hate putting people in that position.'

'But you do it. Because the world needs it. You can't always be perfect.'

'It's fucking hard.'

'Onto the next one, Lars.'

'A good man died.'

'And took seventeen pieces of shit with him. How are those odds?'

'Not good enough. I want 17-0.'

'Then get back to work. Jason King. Will Slater. James Xu. Look at what your agents are doing. Look at what you've achieved in three short years. Don't ever take your foot off the pedal. You're making too much progress to ever consider anything otherwise.'

'I'll send King after Ben Ware. He'll get rid of him.'

'Okay. I'll keep you posted on Ware's whereabouts.'

'Good. Because King's hungry. And he needs to eat.'

'Ware might have help. He hired fourteen men in Bhutan. He must have the bankroll to acquire more.'

'Somehow I think Jason King won't be too bothered by that.'

'So I've heard.'

'Keep me posted.'

'Get some rest, Lars. Griffin didn't die for no reason. He would have been content.'

'You can't know that.'

'Yes I can.'

The man on the other end of the line ended the call. Lars paused with the dead receiver against his ear for a few beats, thinking long and hard about a man named Colt Griffin who had shouldered an impossible burden without hesitation. As chief handler for Black Force, Lars spent most of his life around people of Griffin's calibre, and it never failed to astonish him just what certain individuals were capable of.

He realised he couldn't dwell on the sacrifice for long. In truth he'd been expecting Griffin to wind up dead. He didn't think the man had a hope of succeeding, but he had to attempt something in the face of such horrific circumstances.

Colt Griffin had delivered more than anyone had ever expected.

Actually, no-one had expected a thing, Lars thought.

No-one had known. Deniability was one of the most important aspects of Black Force's existence, and as such what Colt Griffin had done would never be officially acknowledged. There would be no posthumous medals to receive, or noble burials to take part in. If Lars had it his way, the entire nation would stop to honour what Griffin had done.

But instead, he would be quietly shifted into the ranks of the men lost on black operations across the globe.

But he could rest easy, because he'd accomplished the impossible.

All of them could.

Lars Crawford went back to bed, wondering what madness the next day would bring. The world of black operations held no time for remorse or reflection. A horrifying situation would crop up shortly, and someone would need to answer the call.

Lars slept soundly, knowing that his operatives would rise to the occasion.

They always did.

MORE BLACK FORCE SHORTS COMING SOON...

BOOKS BY MATT ROGERS

THE JASON KING SERIES

Isolated (Book 1)

Imprisoned (Book 2)

Reloaded (Book 3)

Betrayed (Book 4)

Corrupted (Book 5)

Hunted (Book 6)

THE JASON KING FILES

Cartel (Book 1)

Warrior (Book 2)

Savages (Book 3)

THE WILL SLATER SERIES

Wolf (Book 1)

Lion (Book 2)

BLACK FORCE SHORTS

The Victor (Book 1)

The Chimera (Book 2)

Join the Reader's Group and get a free 200-page book by Matt Rogers!

Sign up for a free copy of '**HARD IMPACT**'.
Meet Jason King — another member of Black Force.

Experience King's most dangerous mission — action-packed insanity in the heart of the Amazon Rainforest.

No spam guaranteed.

Just click here.

ABOUT THE AUTHOR

Matt Rogers grew up in Melbourne, Australia as a voracious reader, relentlessly devouring thrillers and mysteries in his spare time. Now, he writes full-time. His novels are action-packed and fast-paced. Dive into the Jason King Series to get started with his collection.

Visit his website:

www.mattrogersbooks.com

Visit his Amazon page:

amazon.com/author/mattrogers23

Made in the USA
Columbia, SC
23 March 2018